NANCY DREW

DREW
girl detective ®

PAPERCUTZ™

NANCY DREW
girl detective®

NANCY
DREW
girl detective
#1
BASED ON THE SERIES BY CAROLYN KEENE
Stefan PETRUCHA • Sho MURASE
PAPERCUTZ

Graphic Novels
Available from Papercutz

#1 The Demon of River Heights
#2 Writ In Stone
#3 The Haunted Dollhouse
#4 The Girl Who Wasn't There
(coming February 2006)

$7.95 each in paperback
$12.95 each in hardcover

ALL-NEW STORY FULL-COLOR GRAPHIC NOVEL
NANCY
DREW
girl detective
#3
BASED ON THE SERIES BY CAROLYN KEENE
Stefan PETRUCHA
Sho MURASE
PAPERCUTZ

NANCY
DREW
girl detective
#4
BASED ON THE SERIES BY CAROLYN KEENE
Stefan PETRUCHA • Sho MURASE
PAPERCUTZ

Please add $3.00 for postage and handling for the first book, add $1.00 for each additional book.

Send for our catalog:
Papercutz
555 Eighth Avenue, Suite 1202
New York, NY 10018
www.papercutz.com

NANCY
#2 DREW
girl detective ®

Writ In Stone

STEFAN PETRUCHA • Writer
SHO MURASE • Artist
with 3D CG elements by RACHEL ITO
Based on the series by
CAROLYN KEENE

PAPERCUTZ™
New York

Writ In Stone
STEFAN PETRUCHA – Writer
SHO MURASE – Artist
with 3D CG elements by RACHEL ITO
BRYAN SENKA – Letterer
CARLOS JOSE GUZMAN
SHO MURASE
Colorists
JIM SALICRUP
Editor-in-Chief

ISBN 10: 1-59707-002-5 paperback edition
ISBN 13: 978-1-59707-002-7 paperback edition
ISBN 10: 1-59707-006-8 hardcover edition
ISBN 13: 978-1-59707-006-5 hardcover edition

Printed in China.

10   9   8   7   6   5   4   3   2

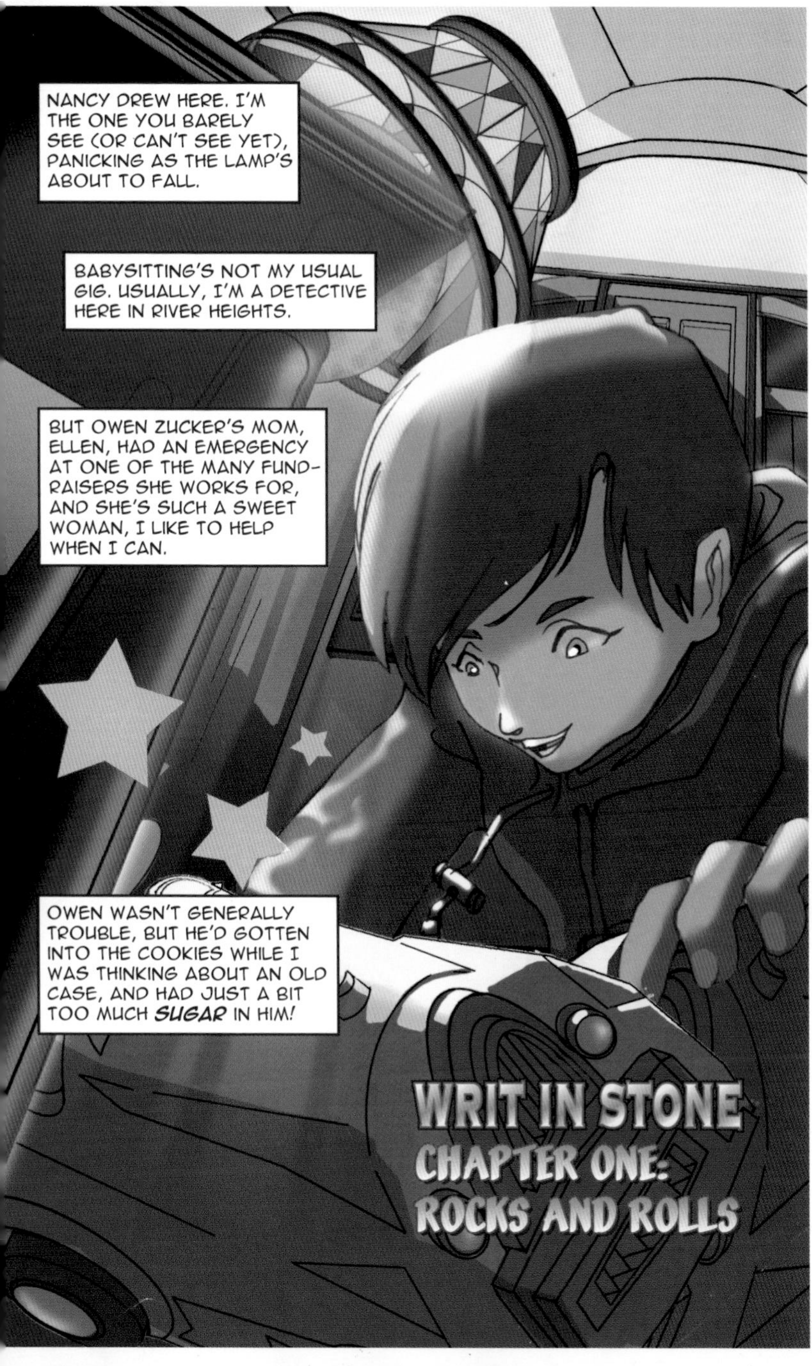

NANCY DREW HERE. I'M THE ONE YOU BARELY SEE (OR CAN'T SEE YET), PANICKING AS THE LAMP'S ABOUT TO FALL.
BABYSITTING'S NOT MY USUAL GIG. USUALLY, I'M A DETECTIVE HERE IN RIVER HEIGHTS.
BUT OWEN ZUCKER'S MOM, ELLEN, HAD AN EMERGENCY AT ONE OF THE MANY FUND-RAISERS SHE WORKS FOR, AND SHE'S SUCH A SWEET WOMAN, I LIKE TO HELP WHEN I CAN.
OWEN WASN'T GENERALLY TROUBLE, BUT HE'D GOTTEN INTO THE COOKIES WHILE I WAS THINKING ABOUT AN OLD CASE, AND HAD JUST A BIT TOO MUCH *SUGAR* IN HIM!
WRIT IN STONE
CHAPTER ONE: ROCKS AND ROLLS

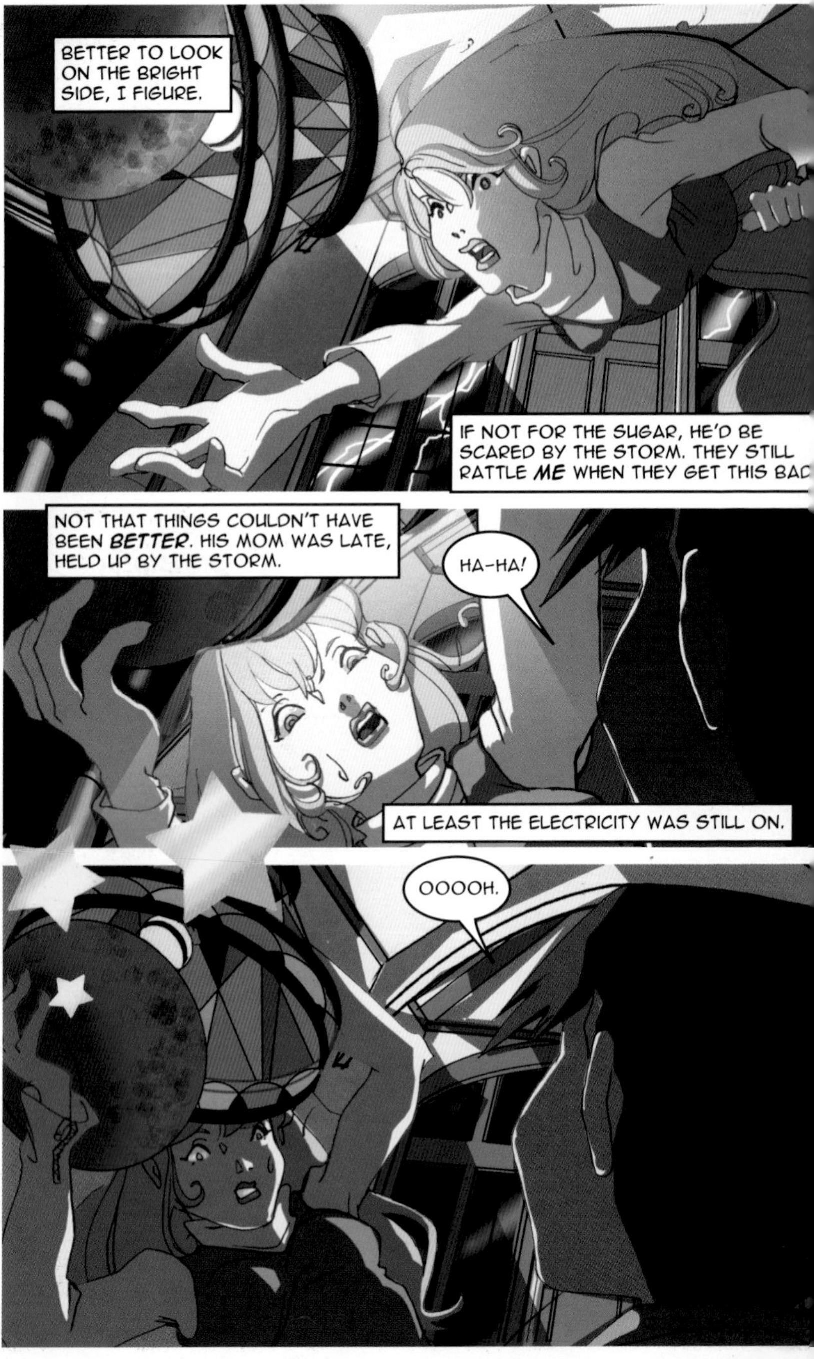
BETTER TO LOOK ON THE BRIGHT SIDE, I FIGURE.
IF NOT FOR THE SUGAR, HE'D BE SCARED BY THE STORM. THEY STILL RATTLE ME WHEN THEY GET THIS BAD
NOT THAT THINGS COULDN'T HAVE BEEN BETTER. HIS MOM WAS LATE, HELD UP BY THE STORM.
HA-HA!
AT LEAST THE ELECTRICITY WAS STILL ON.
OOOOH.

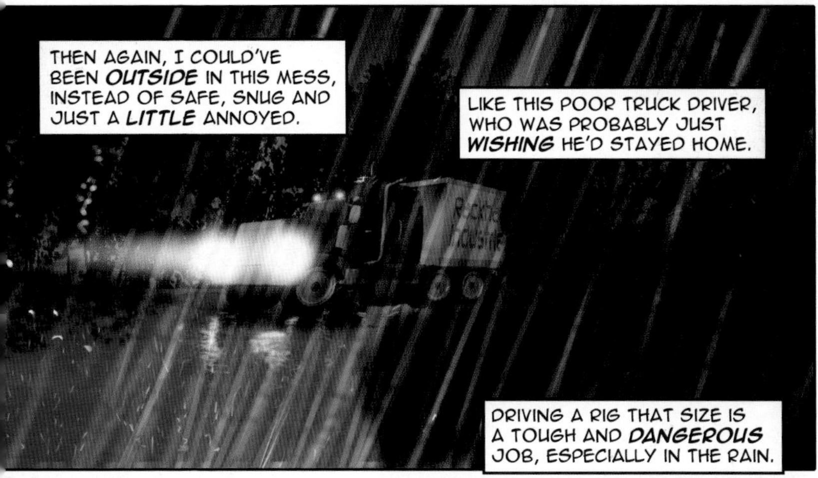
THEN AGAIN, I COULD'VE BEEN *OUTSIDE* IN THIS MESS, INSTEAD OF SAFE, SNUG AND JUST A *LITTLE* ANNOYED.
LIKE THIS POOR TRUCK DRIVER, WHO WAS PROBABLY JUST *WISHING* HE'D STAYED HOME.
DRIVING A RIG THAT SIZE IS A TOUGH AND *DANGEROUS* JOB, ESPECIALLY IN THE RAIN.

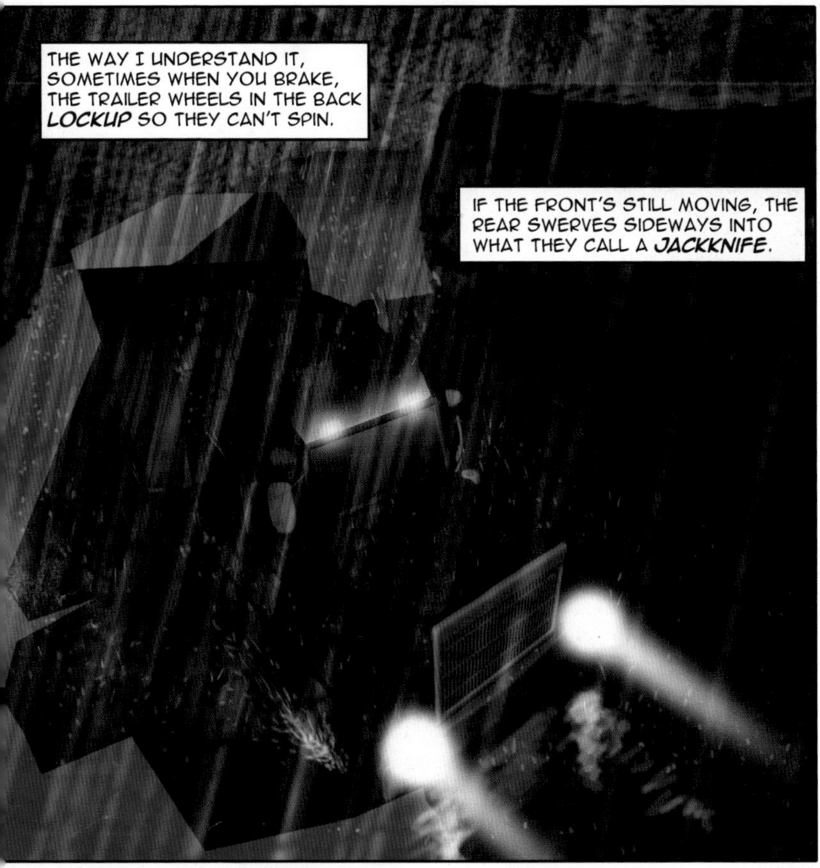
THE WAY I UNDERSTAND IT, SOMETIMES WHEN YOU BRAKE, THE TRAILER WHEELS IN THE BACK *LOCKUP* SO THEY CAN'T SPIN.
IF THE FRONT'S STILL MOVING, THE REAR SWERVES SIDEWAYS INTO WHAT THEY CALL A *JACKKNIFE*.

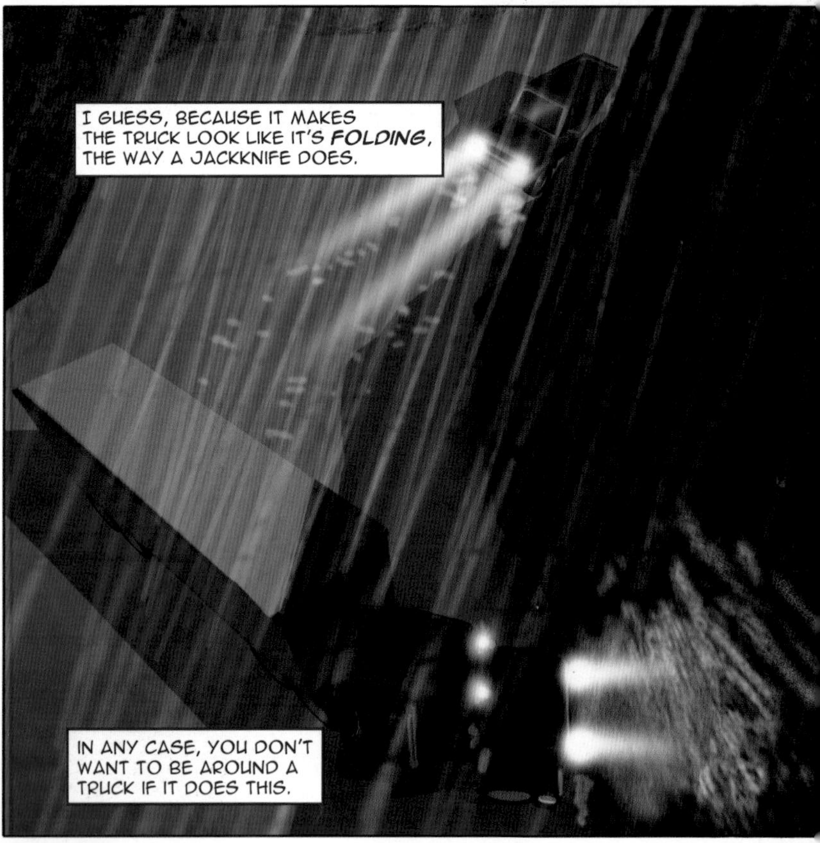
I GUESS, BECAUSE IT MAKES THE TRUCK LOOK LIKE IT'S *FOLDING*, THE WAY A JACKKNIFE DOES.
IN ANY CASE, YOU DON'T WANT TO BE AROUND A TRUCK IF IT DOES THIS.

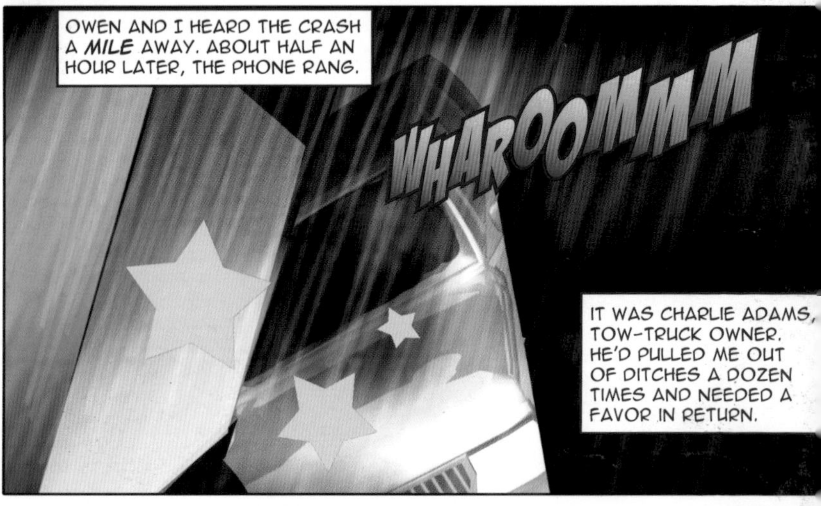
OWEN AND I HEARD THE CRASH A *MILE* AWAY. ABOUT HALF AN HOUR LATER, THE PHONE RANG.
WHAROOMMM
IT WAS CHARLIE ADAMS, TOW-TRUCK OWNER. HE'D PULLED ME OUT OF DITCHES A DOZEN TIMES AND NEEDED A FAVOR IN RETURN.

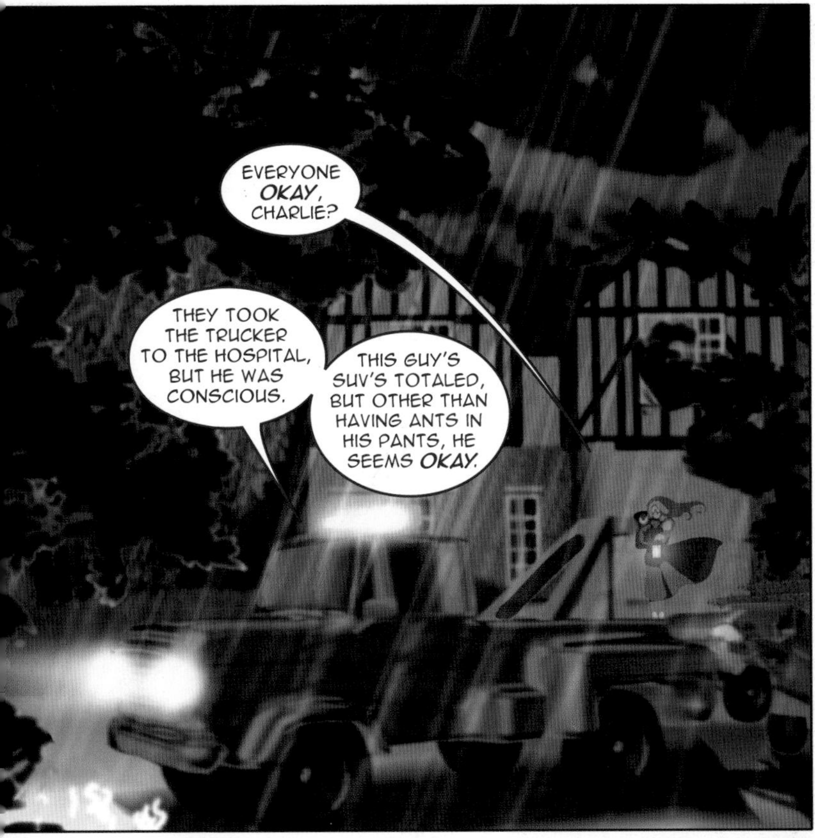
EVERYONE OKAY, CHARLIE?
THEY TOOK THE TRUCKER TO THE HOSPITAL, BUT HE WAS CONSCIOUS.
THIS GUY'S SUV'S TOTALED, BUT OTHER THAN HAVING ANTS IN HIS PANTS, HE SEEMS OKAY.

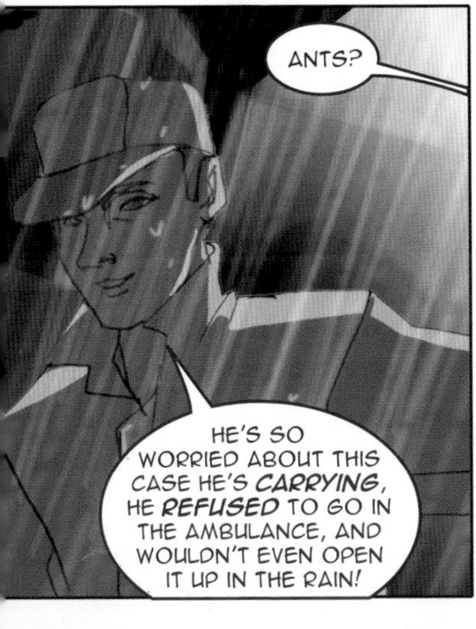
ANTS?
HE'S SO WORRIED ABOUT THIS CASE HE'S CARRYING, HE REFUSED TO GO IN THE AMBULANCE, AND WOULDN'T EVEN OPEN IT UP IN THE RAIN!

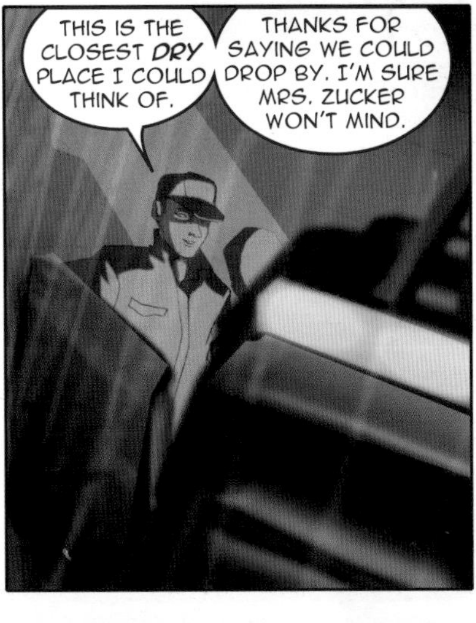
THIS IS THE CLOSEST DRY PLACE I COULD THINK OF.
THANKS FOR SAYING WE COULD DROP BY. I'M SURE MRS. ZUCKER WON'T MIND.

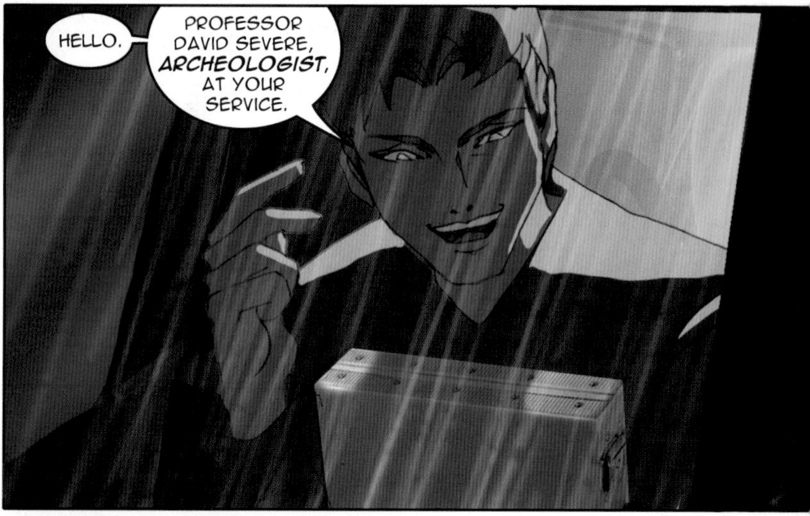
HELLO.
PROFESSOR DAVID SEVERE, *ARCHEOLOGIST*, AT YOUR SERVICE.

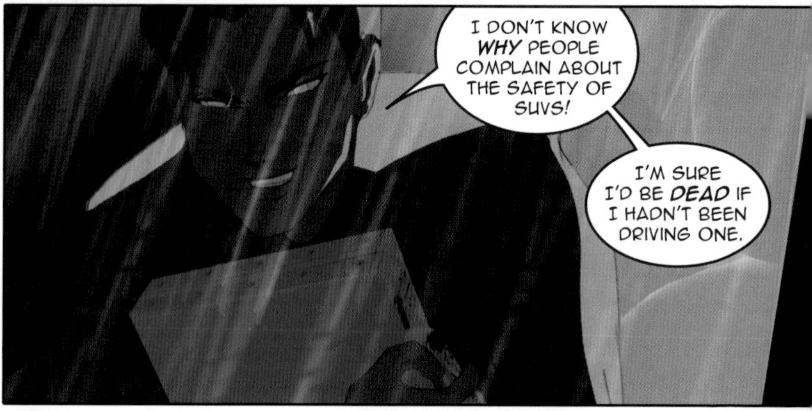
I DON'T KNOW *WHY* PEOPLE COMPLAIN ABOUT THE SAFETY OF SUVS!
I'M SURE I'D BE *DEAD* IF I HADN'T BEEN DRIVING ONE.

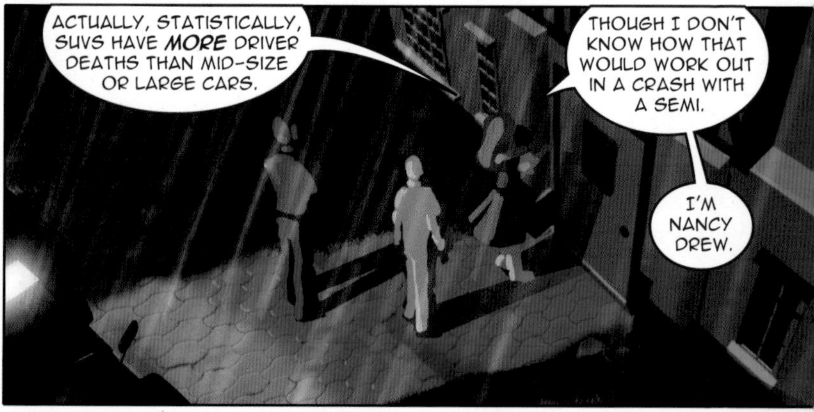
ACTUALLY, STATISTICALLY, SUVS HAVE *MORE* DRIVER DEATHS THAN MID-SIZE OR LARGE CARS.
THOUGH I DON'T KNOW HOW THAT WOULD WORK OUT IN A CRASH WITH A SEMI.
I'M NANCY DREW.

DREW, EH? YOU'RE THAT GIRL-DETECTIVE, AREN'T YOU? THIS IS *FORTUNATE.*

AN INQUIRING MIND LIKE YOURS SHOULD HAVE A PARTICULAR INTEREST IN SEEING...

THIS!

GASP!

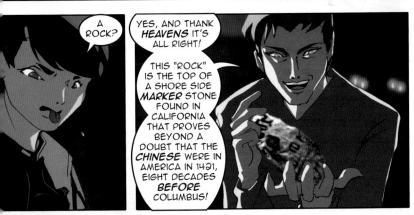

A ROCK?

YES, AND THANK *HEAVENS* IT'S ALL RIGHT!

THIS "ROCK" IS THE TOP OF A SHORE SIDE *MARKER* STONE FOUND IN CALIFORNIA THAT PROVES BEYOND A DOUBT THAT THE *CHINESE* WERE IN AMERICA IN 1421, EIGHT DECADES *BEFORE* COLUMBUS!

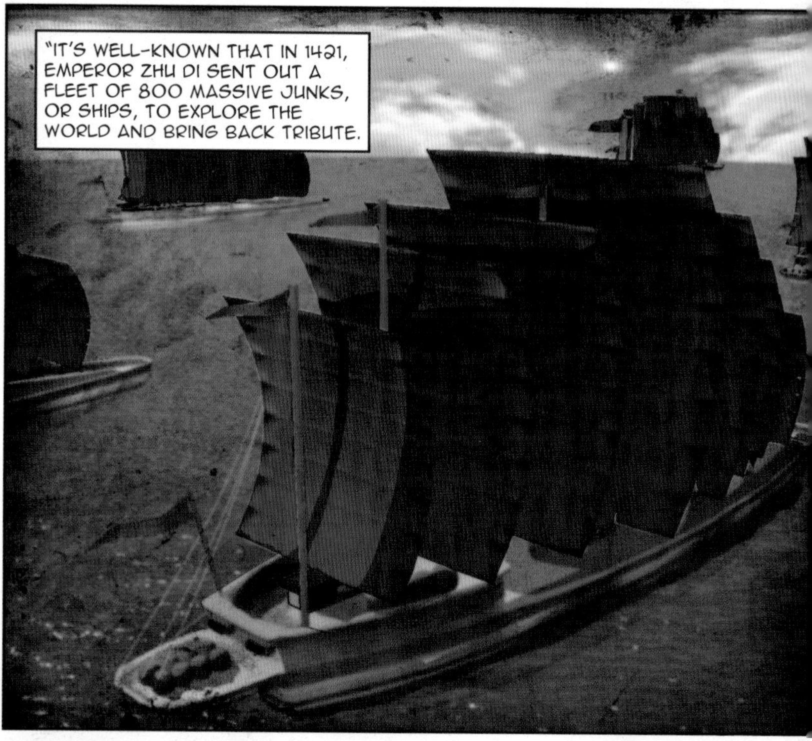
"IT'S WELL-KNOWN THAT IN 1421, EMPEROR ZHU DI SENT OUT A FLEET OF 800 MASSIVE JUNKS, OR SHIPS, TO EXPLORE THE WORLD AND BRING BACK TRIBUTE.

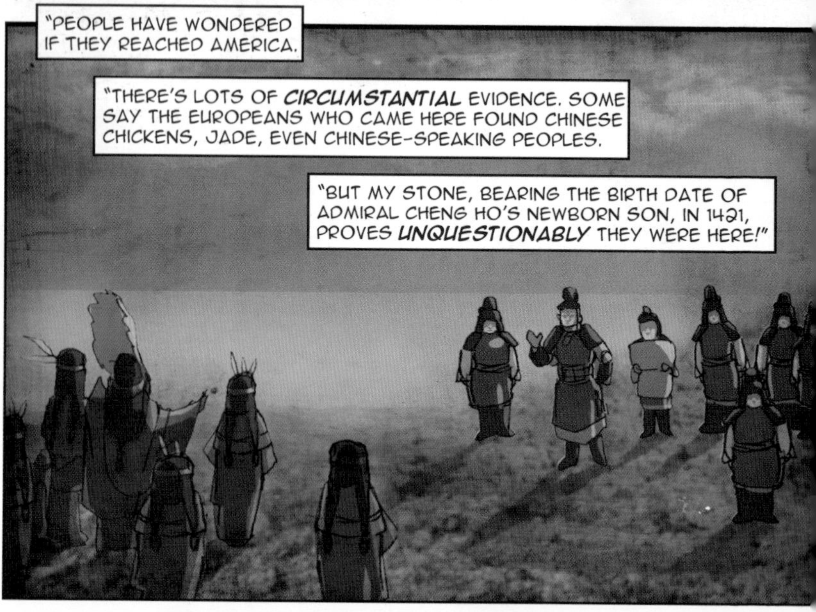
"PEOPLE HAVE WONDERED IF THEY REACHED AMERICA.
"THERE'S LOTS OF *CIRCUMSTANTIAL* EVIDENCE. SOME SAY THE EUROPEANS WHO CAME HERE FOUND CHINESE CHICKENS, JADE, EVEN CHINESE-SPEAKING PEOPLES.
"BUT MY STONE, BEARING THE BIRTH DATE OF ADMIRAL CHENG HO'S NEWBORN SON, IN 1421, PROVES ***UNQUESTIONABLY*** THEY WERE HERE!"

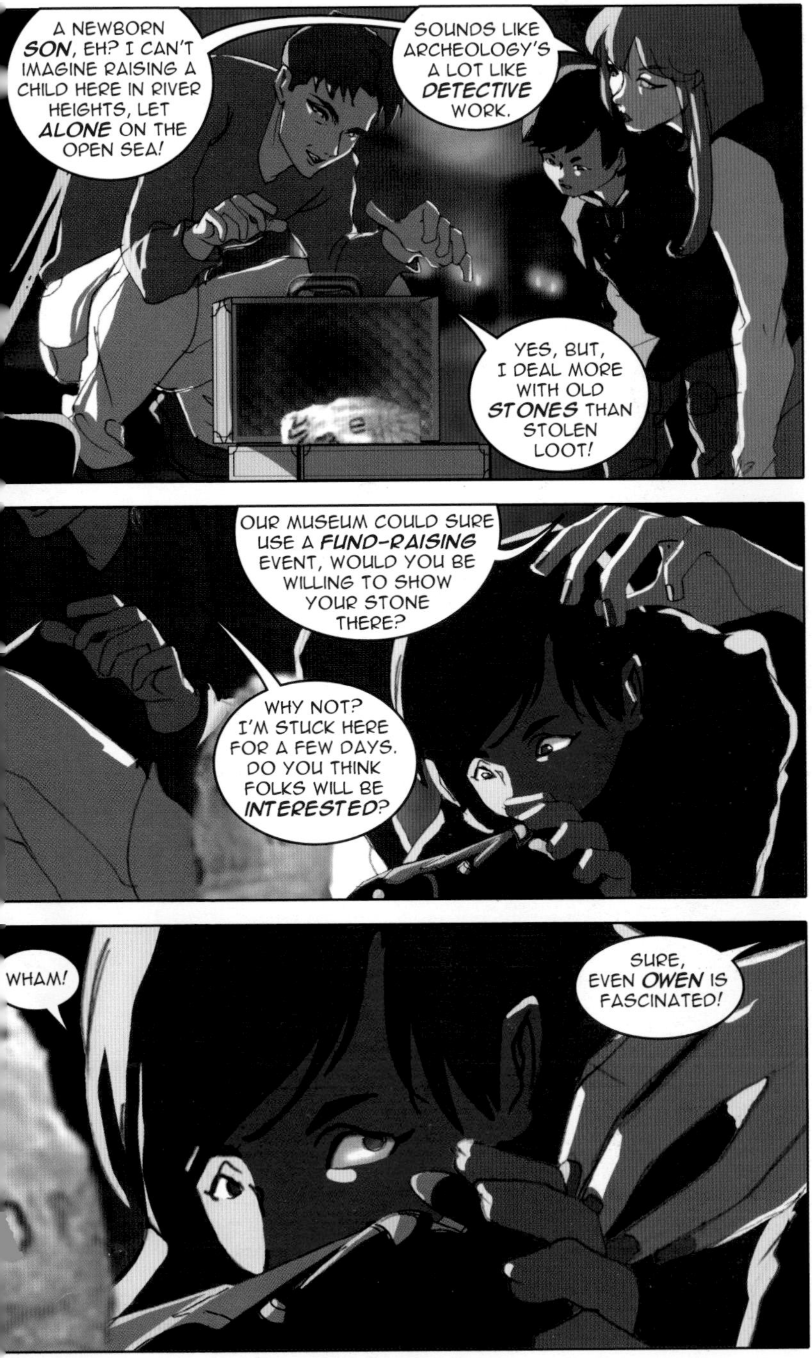
A NEWBORN SON, EH? I CAN'T IMAGINE RAISING A CHILD HERE IN RIVER HEIGHTS, LET ALONE ON THE OPEN SEA!
SOUNDS LIKE ARCHEOLOGY'S A LOT LIKE DETECTIVE WORK.
YES, BUT, I DEAL MORE WITH OLD STONES THAN STOLEN LOOT!
OUR MUSEUM COULD SURE USE A FUND-RAISING EVENT, WOULD YOU BE WILLING TO SHOW YOUR STONE THERE?
WHY NOT? I'M STUCK HERE FOR A FEW DAYS. DO YOU THINK FOLKS WILL BE INTERESTED?
WHAM!
SURE, EVEN OWEN IS FASCINATED!

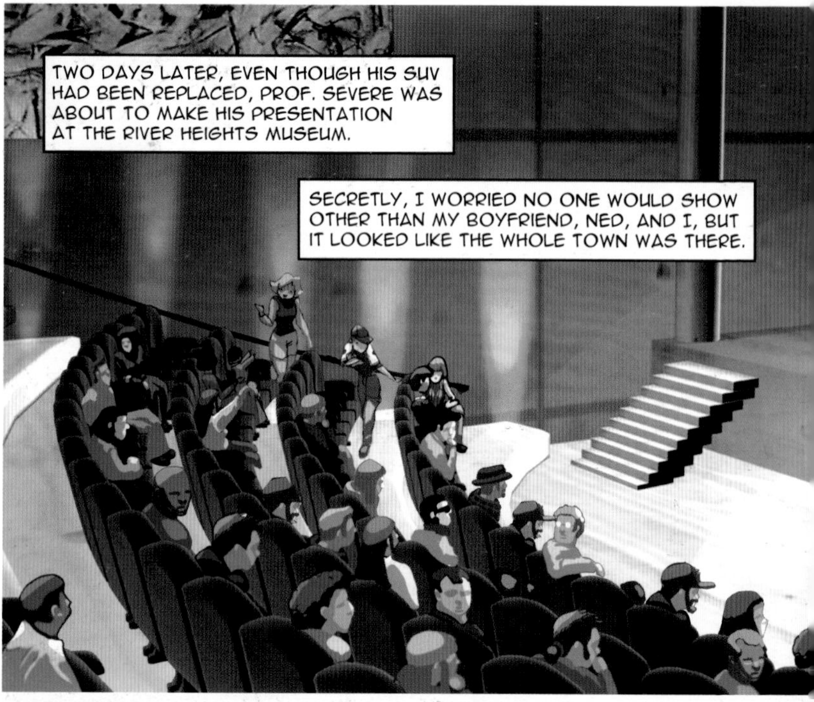
TWO DAYS LATER, EVEN THOUGH HIS SUV HAD BEEN REPLACED, PROF. SEVERE WAS ABOUT TO MAKE HIS PRESENTATION AT THE RIVER HEIGHTS MUSEUM.
SECRETLY, I WORRIED NO ONE WOULD SHOW OTHER THAN MY BOYFRIEND, NED, AND I, BUT IT LOOKED LIKE THE WHOLE TOWN WAS THERE.

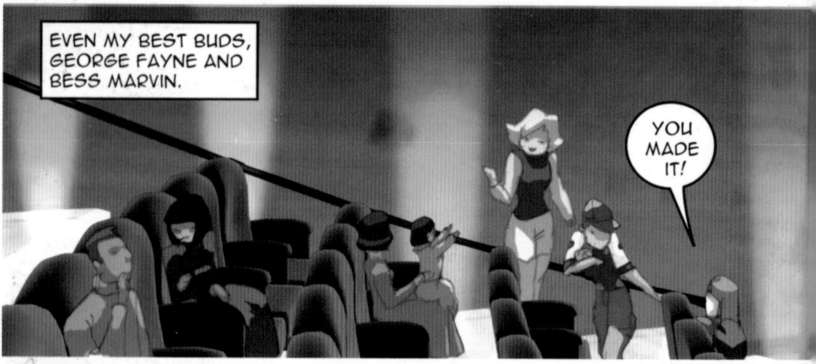
EVEN MY BEST BUDS, GEORGE FAYNE AND BESS MARVIN.
YOU MADE IT!

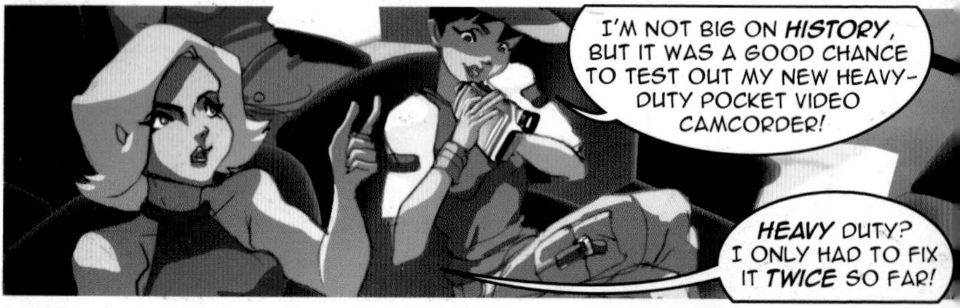
I'M NOT BIG ON *HISTORY*, BUT IT WAS A GOOD CHANCE TO TEST OUT MY NEW HEAVY-DUTY POCKET VIDEO CAMCORDER!
HEAVY DUTY? I ONLY HAD TO FIX IT *TWICE* SO FAR!

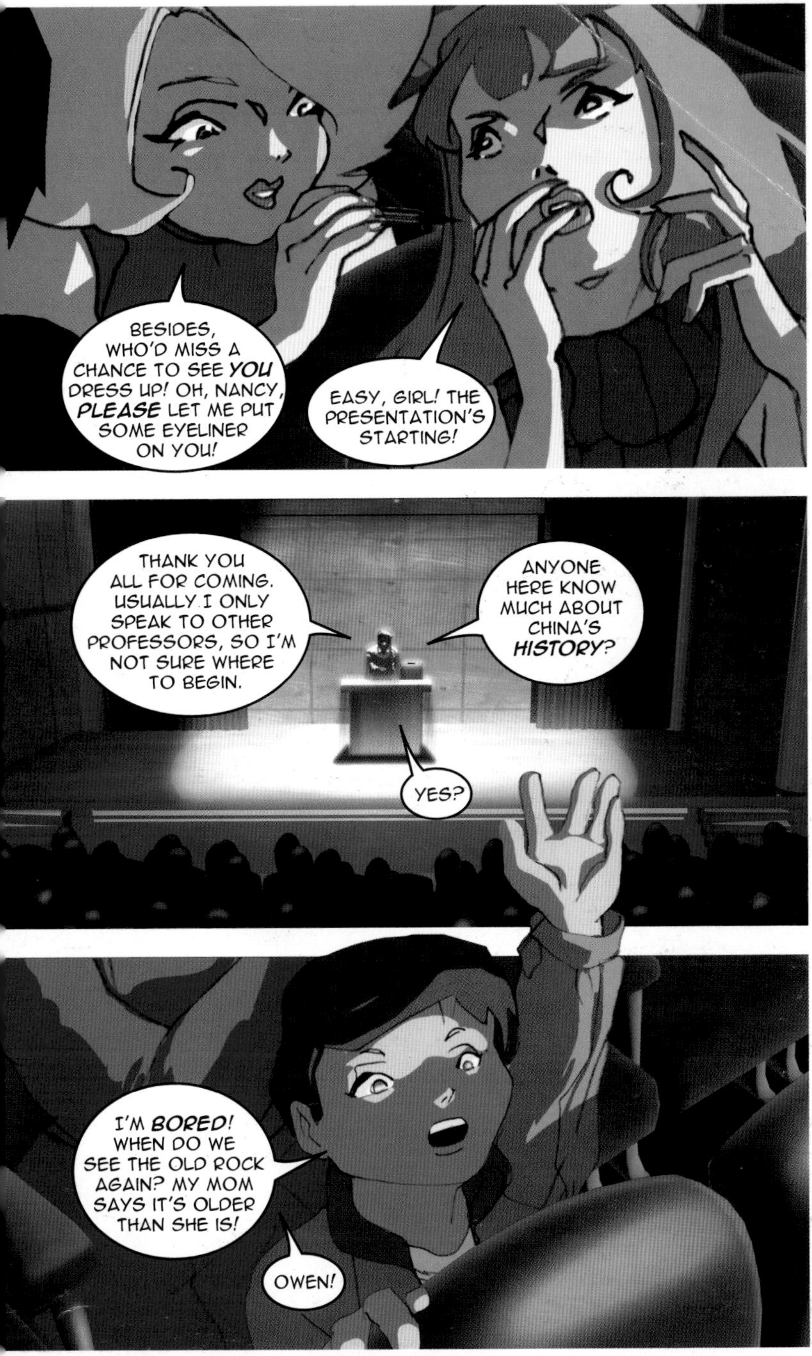
BESIDES, WHO'D MISS A CHANCE TO SEE *YOU* DRESS UP! OH, NANCY, *PLEASE* LET ME PUT SOME EYELINER ON YOU!
EASY, GIRL! THE PRESENTATION'S STARTING!
THANK YOU ALL FOR COMING. USUALLY I ONLY SPEAK TO OTHER PROFESSORS, SO I'M NOT SURE WHERE TO BEGIN.
ANYONE HERE KNOW MUCH ABOUT CHINA'S *HISTORY*?
YES?
I'M *BORED*! WHEN DO WE SEE THE OLD ROCK AGAIN? MY MOM SAYS IT'S OLDER THAN SHE IS!
OWEN!

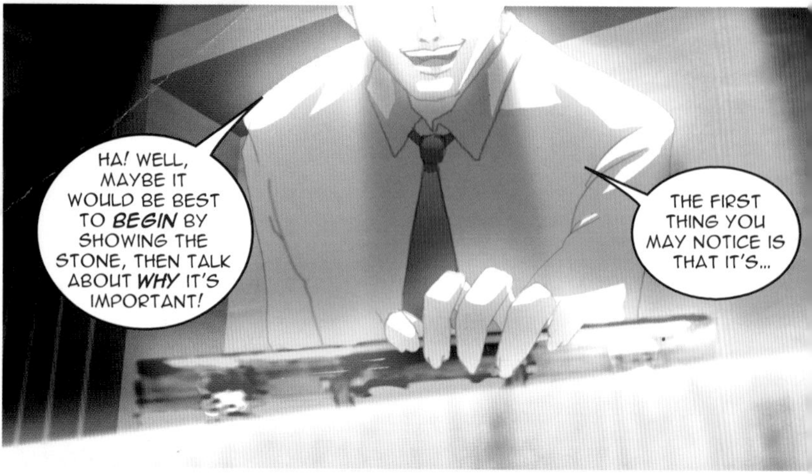
HA! WELL, MAYBE IT WOULD BE BEST TO *BEGIN* BY SHOWING THE STONE, THEN TALK ABOUT *WHY* IT'S IMPORTANT!
THE FIRST THING YOU MAY NOTICE IS THAT IT'S...

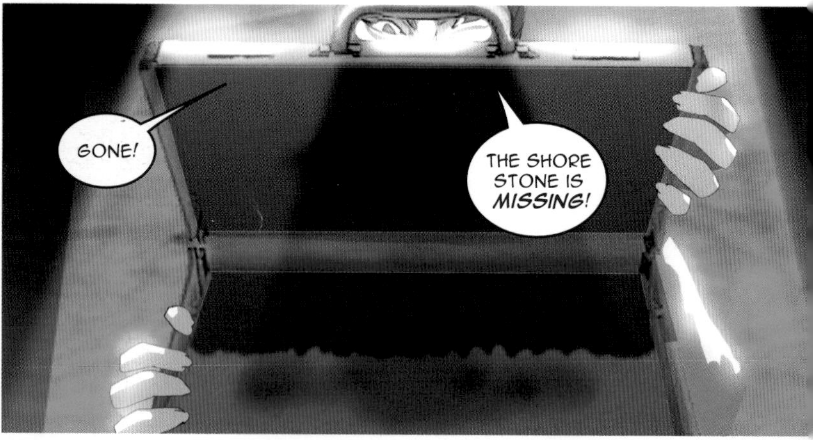
GONE!
THE SHORE STONE IS *MISSING*!

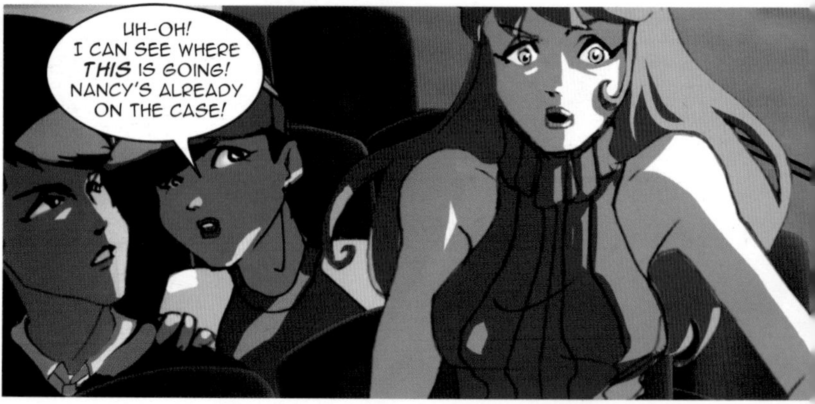
UH-OH! I CAN SEE WHERE *THIS* IS GOING! NANCY'S ALREADY ON THE CASE!

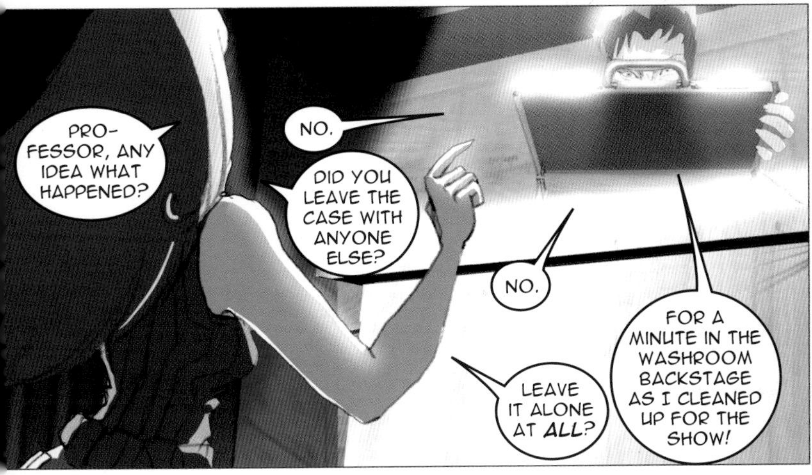
PRO-FESSOR, ANY IDEA WHAT HAPPENED?
NO.
DID YOU LEAVE THE CASE WITH ANYONE ELSE?
NO.
LEAVE IT ALONE AT ALL?
FOR A MINUTE IN THE WASHROOM BACKSTAGE AS I CLEANED UP FOR THE SHOW!

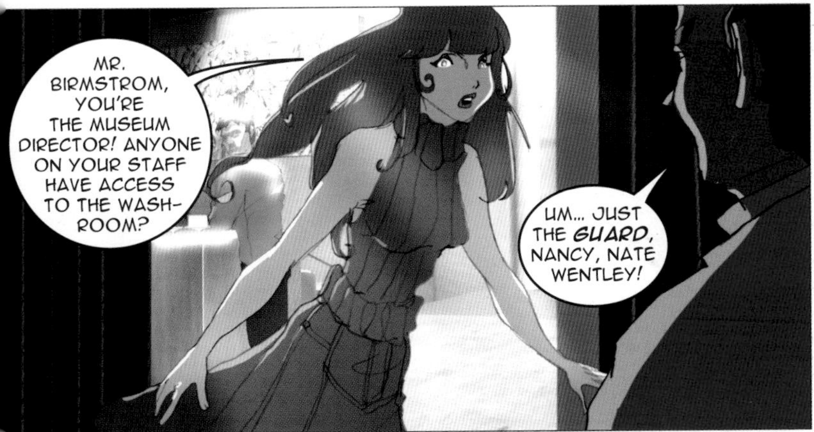
MR. BIRMSTROM, YOU'RE THE MUSEUM DIRECTOR! ANYONE ON YOUR STAFF HAVE ACCESS TO THE WASH-ROOM?
UM... JUST THE GUARD, NANCY, NATE WENTLEY!

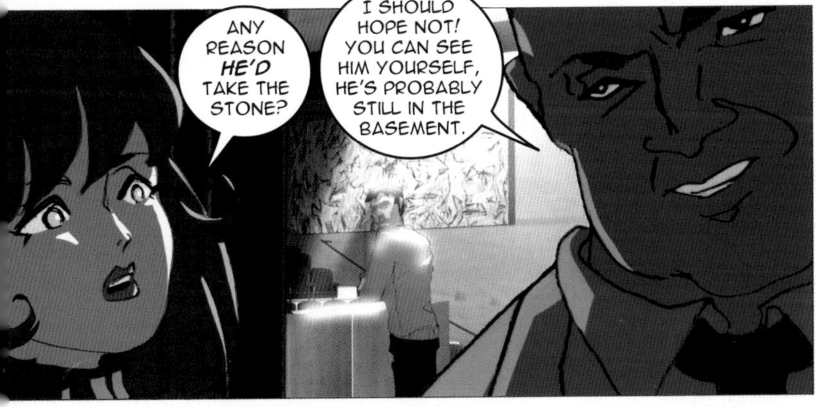
ANY REASON HE'D TAKE THE STONE?
I SHOULD HOPE NOT! YOU CAN SEE HIM YOURSELF, HE'S PROBABLY STILL IN THE BASEMENT.

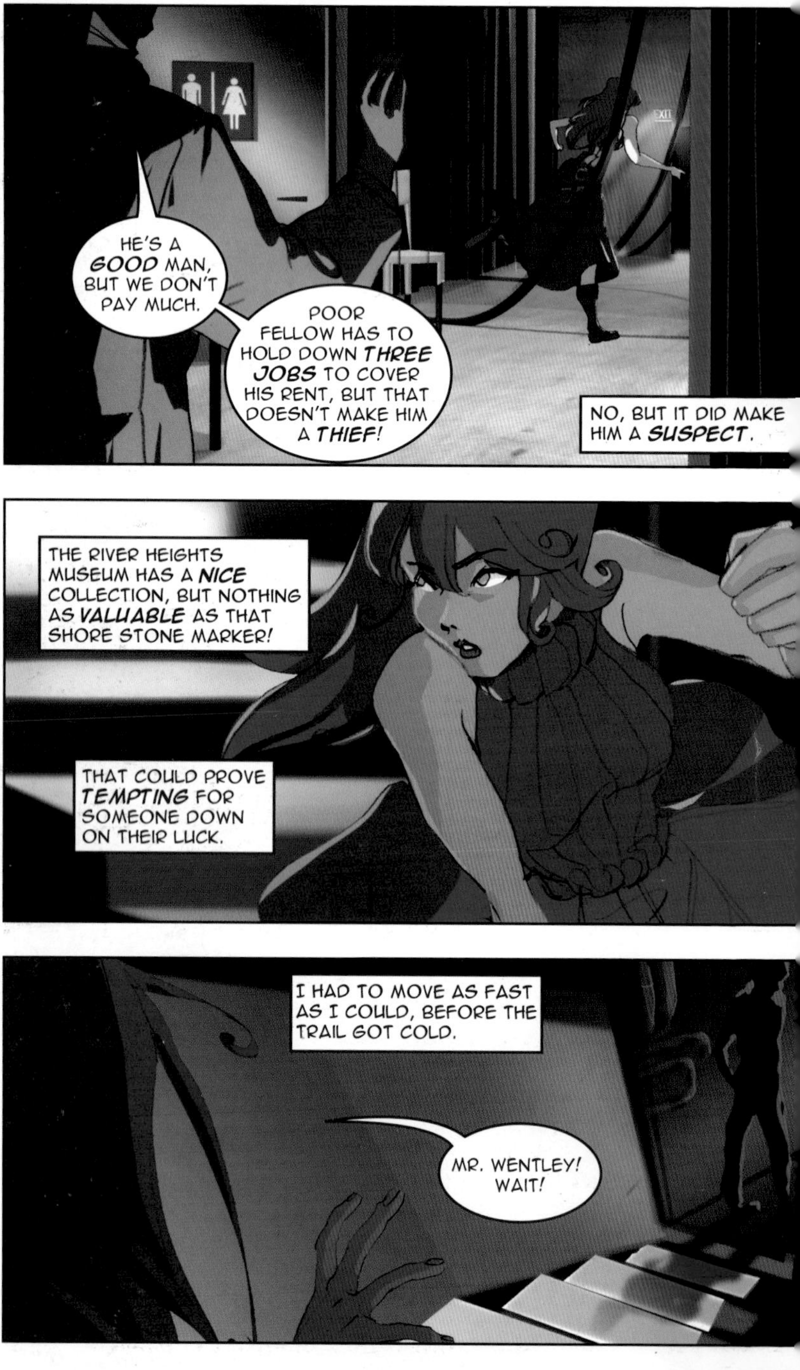
HE'S A GOOD MAN, BUT WE DON'T PAY MUCH.
POOR FELLOW HAS TO HOLD DOWN THREE JOBS TO COVER HIS RENT, BUT THAT DOESN'T MAKE HIM A THIEF!
NO, BUT IT DID MAKE HIM A SUSPECT.
THE RIVER HEIGHTS MUSEUM HAS A NICE COLLECTION, BUT NOTHING AS VALUABLE AS THAT SHORE STONE MARKER!
THAT COULD PROVE TEMPTING FOR SOMEONE DOWN ON THEIR LUCK.
I HAD TO MOVE AS FAST AS I COULD, BEFORE THE TRAIL GOT COLD.
MR. WENTLEY! WAIT!

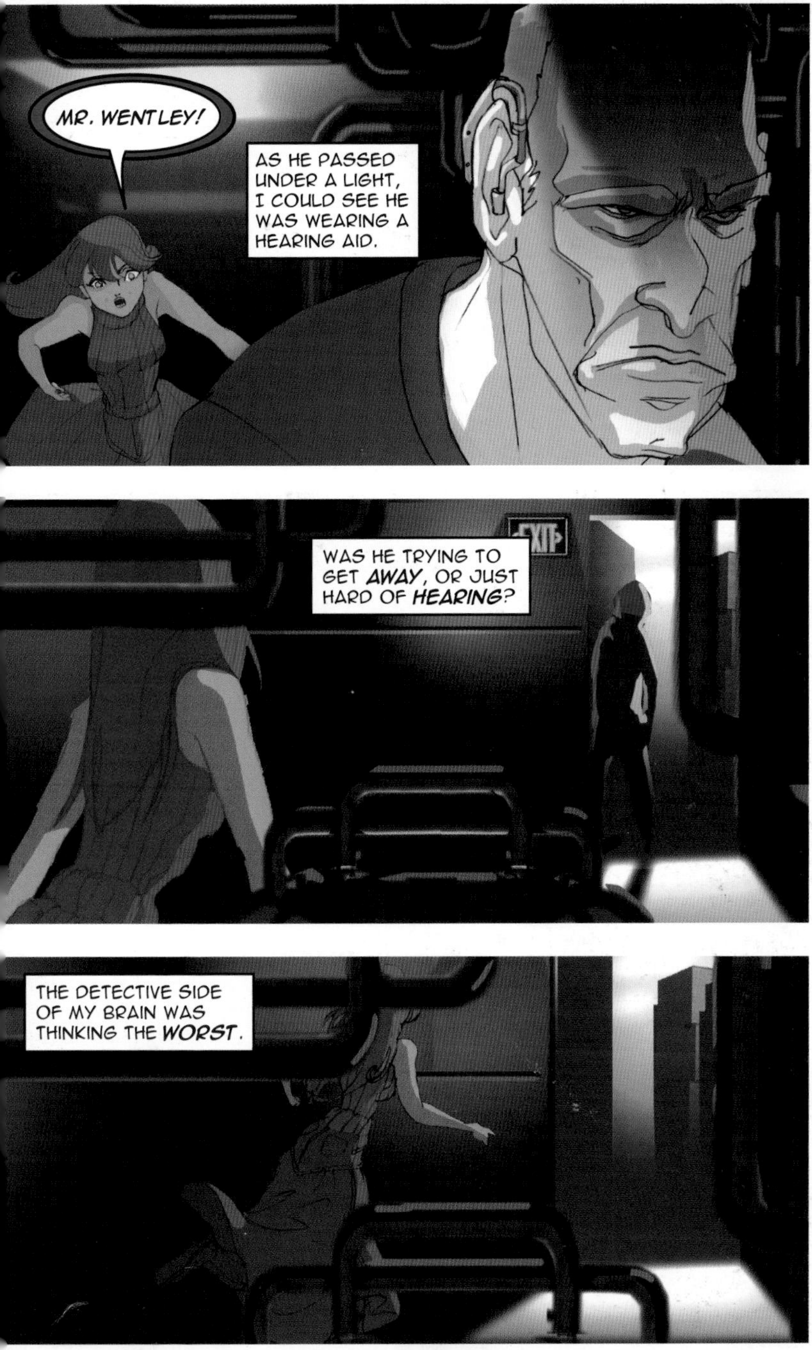
MR. WENTLEY!
AS HE PASSED UNDER A LIGHT, I COULD SEE HE WAS WEARING A HEARING AID.
EXIT
WAS HE TRYING TO GET *AWAY*, OR JUST HARD OF *HEARING*?
THE DETECTIVE SIDE OF MY BRAIN WAS THINKING THE *WORST*.

THE PROBLEM WITH THAT DETECTIVE BRAIN IS THAT WHILE IT'S *GREAT* ON *CRIME* DETAILS...

MR. WENTLEY! PLEASE OPEN THE DOOR! I JUST WANT TO *TALK* TO YOU!

...SOMETIMES IT DOESN'T PAY ATTENTION TO ANYTHING *ELSE* GOING ON.

LIKE WHERE I AM, OR HOW EASY IT MIGHT BE TO *TRAP* ME THERE!

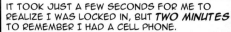

IT TOOK JUST A FEW SECONDS FOR ME TO REALIZE I WAS LOCKED IN, BUT *TWO MINUTES* TO REMEMBER I HAD A CELL PHONE.

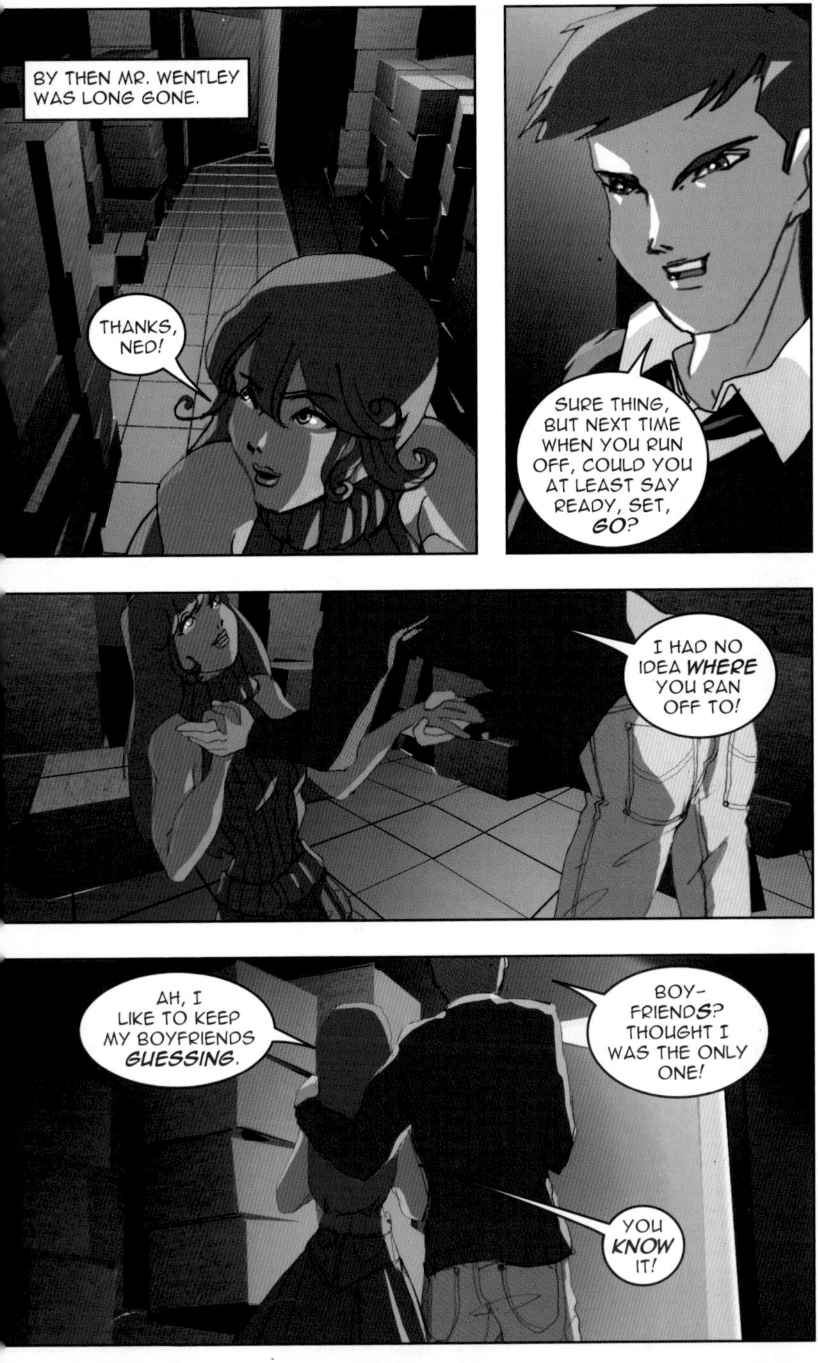
BY THEN MR. WENTLEY WAS LONG GONE.
THANKS, NED!
SURE THING, BUT NEXT TIME WHEN YOU RUN OFF, COULD YOU AT LEAST SAY READY, SET, GO?
I HAD NO IDEA WHERE YOU RAN OFF TO!
AH, I LIKE TO KEEP MY BOYFRIENDS GUESSING.
BOY-FRIENDS? THOUGHT I WAS THE ONLY ONE!
YOU KNOW IT!

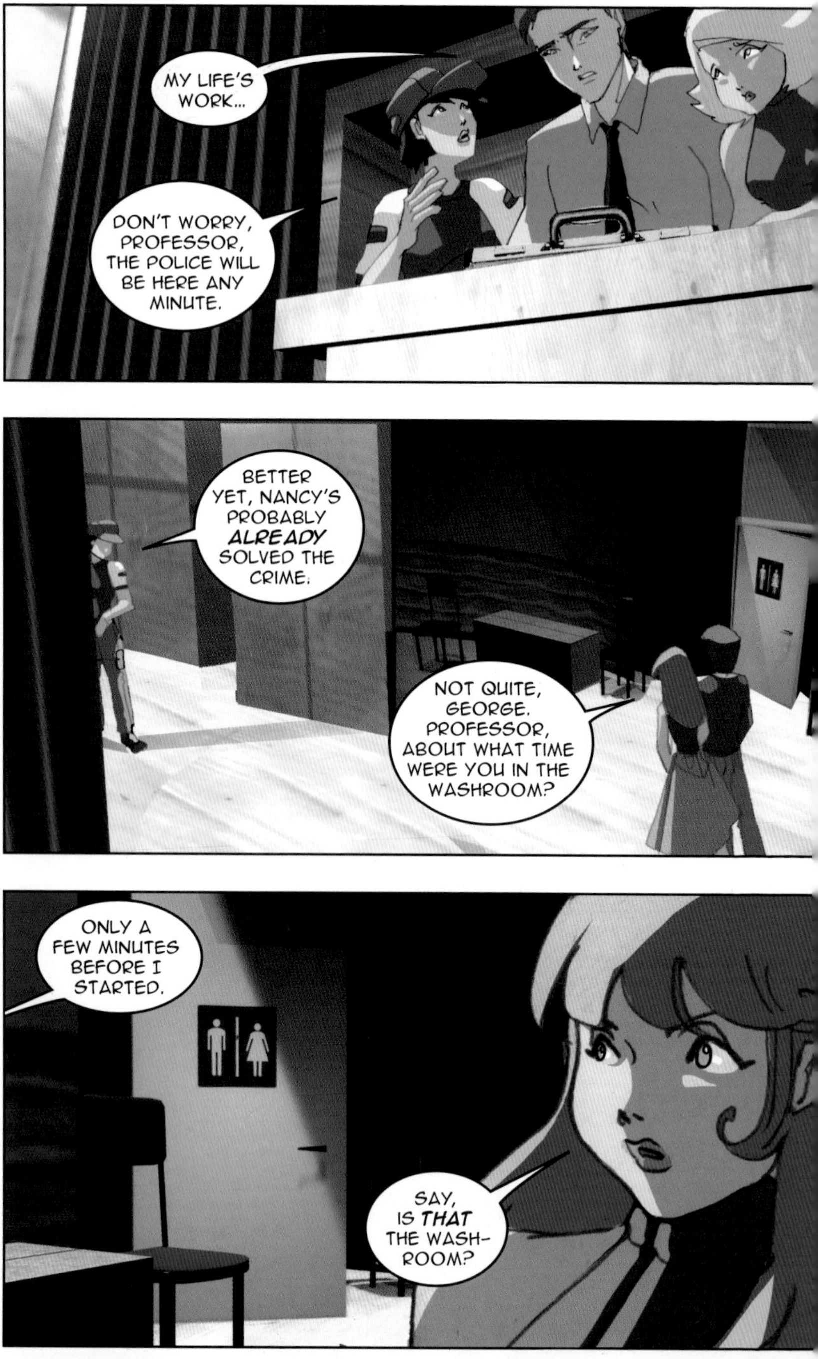
MY LIFE'S WORK...
DON'T WORRY, PROFESSOR, THE POLICE WILL BE HERE ANY MINUTE.
BETTER YET, NANCY'S PROBABLY *ALREADY* SOLVED THE CRIME.
NOT QUITE, GEORGE. PROFESSOR, ABOUT WHAT TIME WERE YOU IN THE WASHROOM?
ONLY A FEW MINUTES BEFORE I STARTED.
SAY, IS *THAT* THE WASH-ROOM?

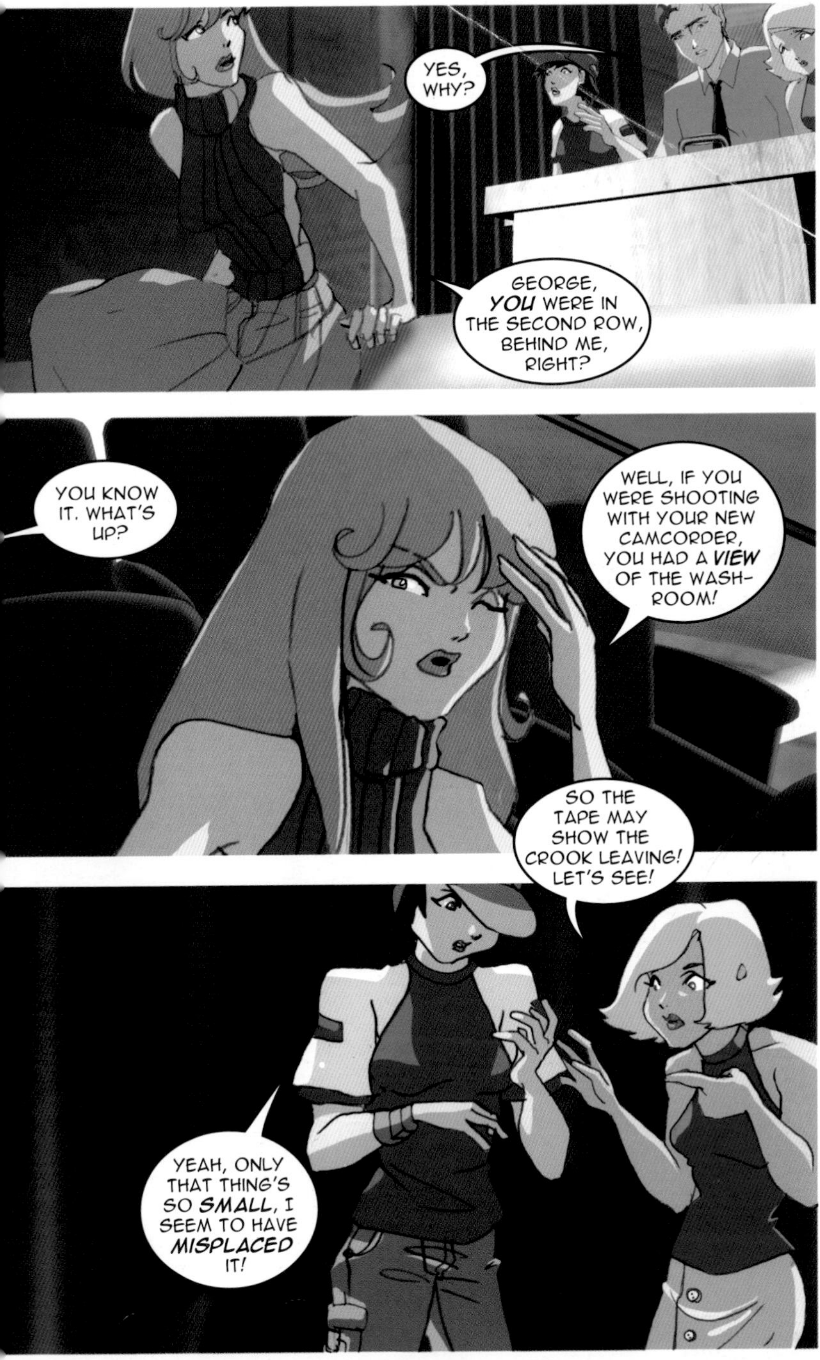
YES, WHY?
GEORGE, YOU WERE IN THE SECOND ROW, BEHIND ME, RIGHT?
YOU KNOW IT. WHAT'S UP?
WELL, IF YOU WERE SHOOTING WITH YOUR NEW CAMCORDER, YOU HAD A VIEW OF THE WASH-ROOM!
SO THE TAPE MAY SHOW THE CROOK LEAVING! LET'S SEE!
YEAH, ONLY THAT THING'S SO SMALL, I SEEM TO HAVE MISPLACED IT!

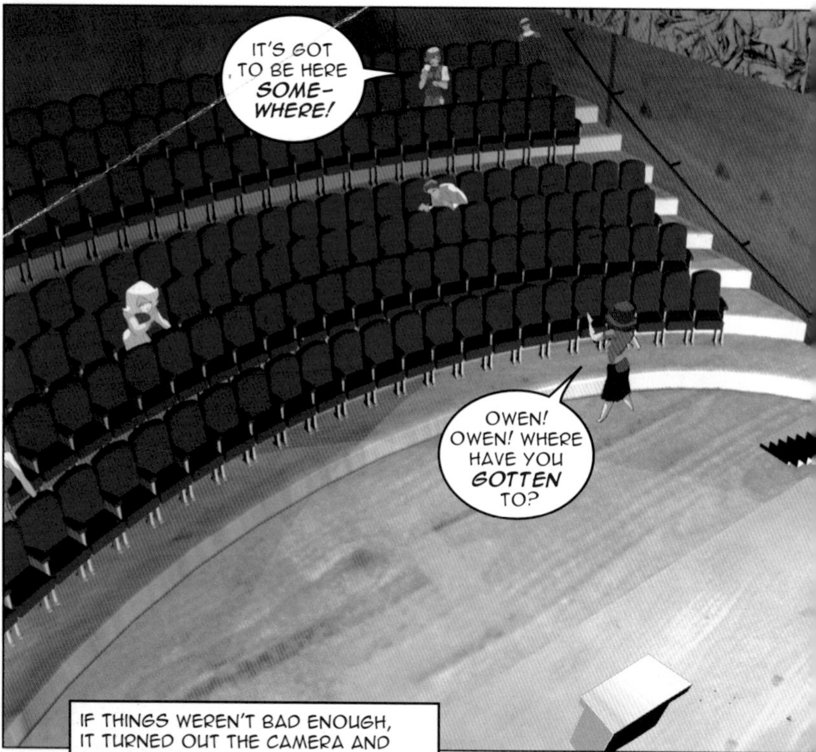
IT'S GOT TO BE HERE *SOME-WHERE!*
OWEN! OWEN! WHERE HAVE YOU *GOTTEN* TO?
IF THINGS WEREN'T BAD ENOUGH, IT TURNED OUT THE CAMERA AND THE SHORE STONE MARKER WEREN'T THE *ONLY* THINGS MISSING...

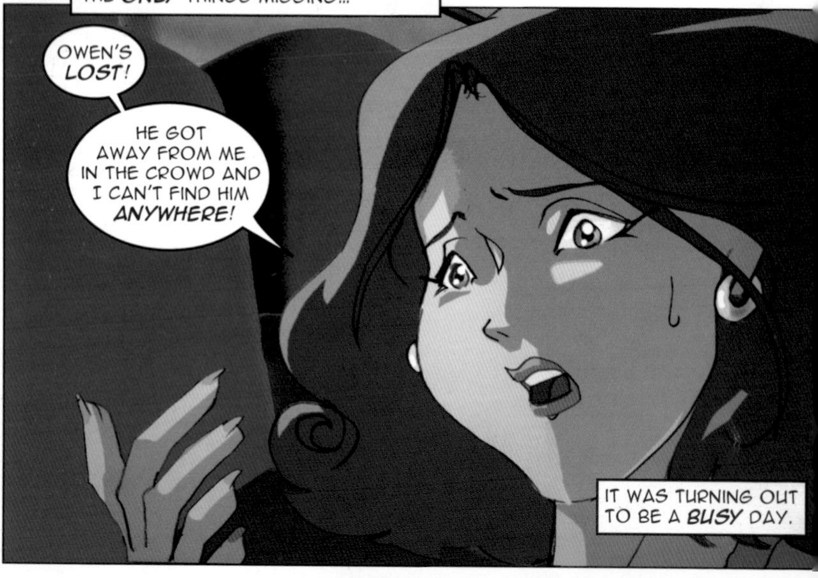
OWEN'S *LOST!*
HE GOT AWAY FROM ME IN THE CROWD AND I CAN'T FIND HIM *ANYWHERE!*
IT WAS TURNING OUT TO BE A *BUSY* DAY.

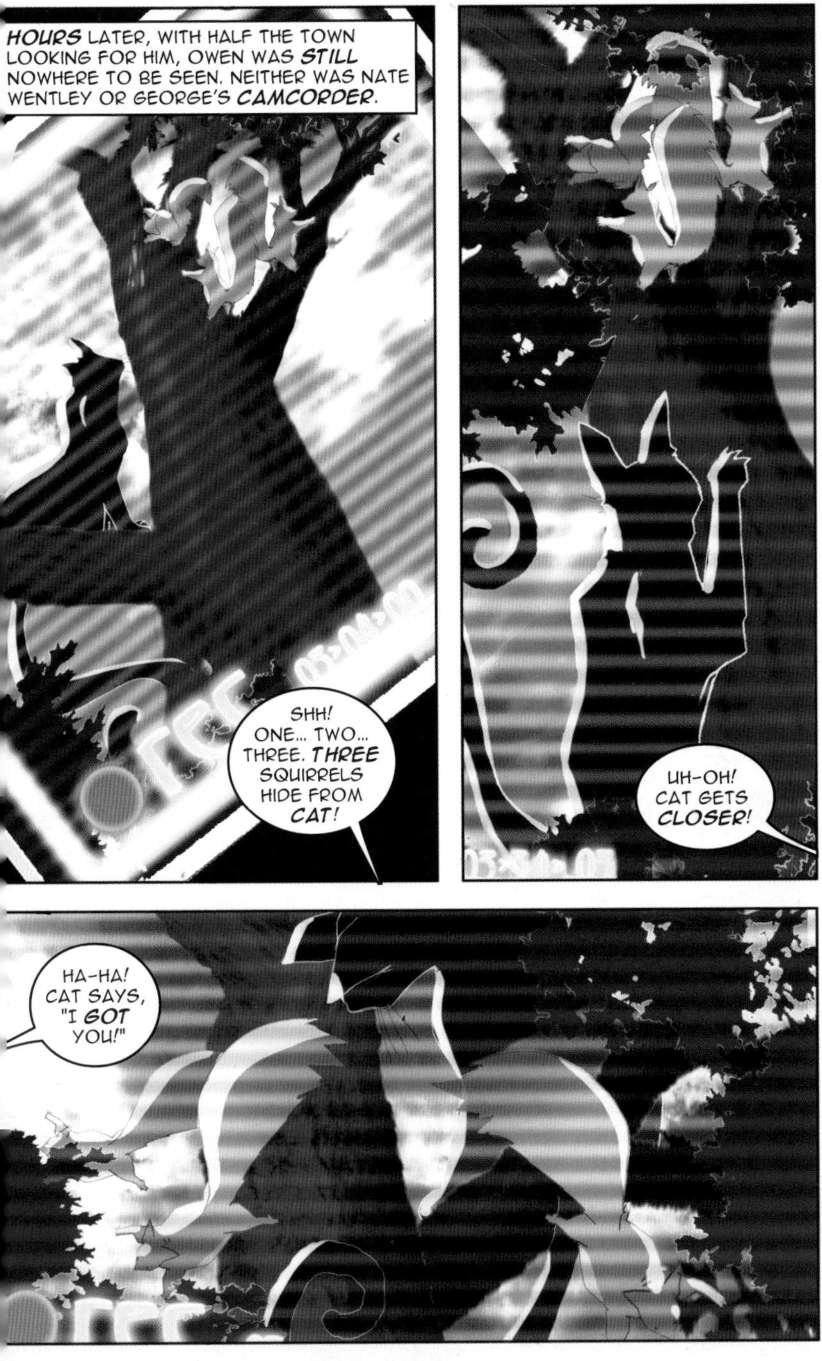
HOURS LATER, WITH HALF THE TOWN LOOKING FOR HIM, OWEN WAS STILL NOWHERE TO BE SEEN. NEITHER WAS NATE WENTLEY OR GEORGE'S CAMCORDER.
SHH! ONE... TWO... THREE. THREE SQUIRRELS HIDE FROM CAT!
UH-OH! CAT GETS CLOSER!
HA-HA! CAT SAYS, "I GOT YOU!"

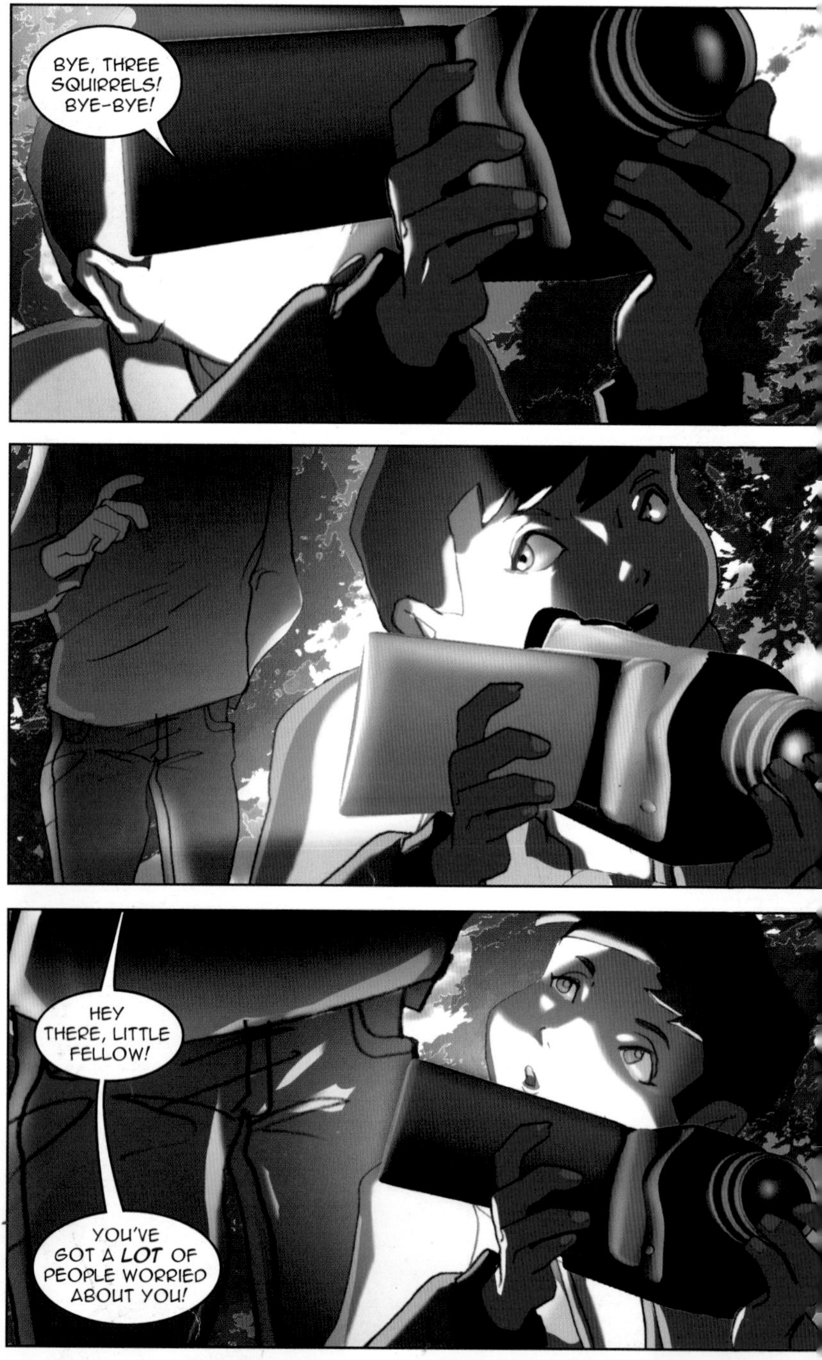
BYE, THREE SQUIRRELS! BYE-BYE!
HEY THERE, LITTLE FELLOW!
YOU'VE GOT A LOT OF PEOPLE WORRIED ABOUT YOU!

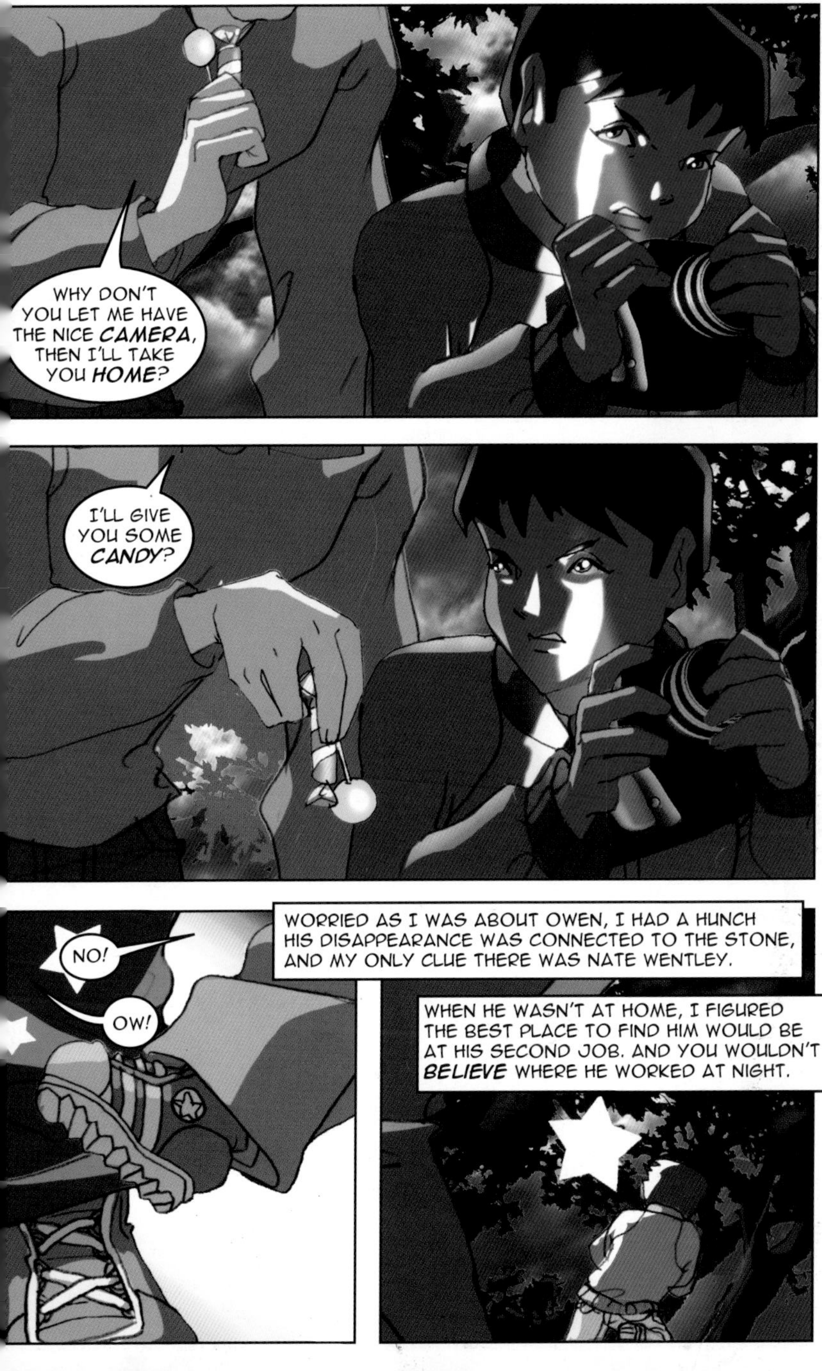
WHY DON'T YOU LET ME HAVE THE NICE CAMERA, THEN I'LL TAKE YOU HOME?
I'LL GIVE YOU SOME CANDY?
NO!
OW!
WORRIED AS I WAS ABOUT OWEN, I HAD A HUNCH HIS DISAPPEARANCE WAS CONNECTED TO THE STONE, AND MY ONLY CLUE THERE WAS NATE WENTLEY.
WHEN HE WASN'T AT HOME, I FIGURED THE BEST PLACE TO FIND HIM WOULD BE AT HIS SECOND JOB. AND YOU WOULDN'T BELIEVE WHERE HE WORKED AT NIGHT.

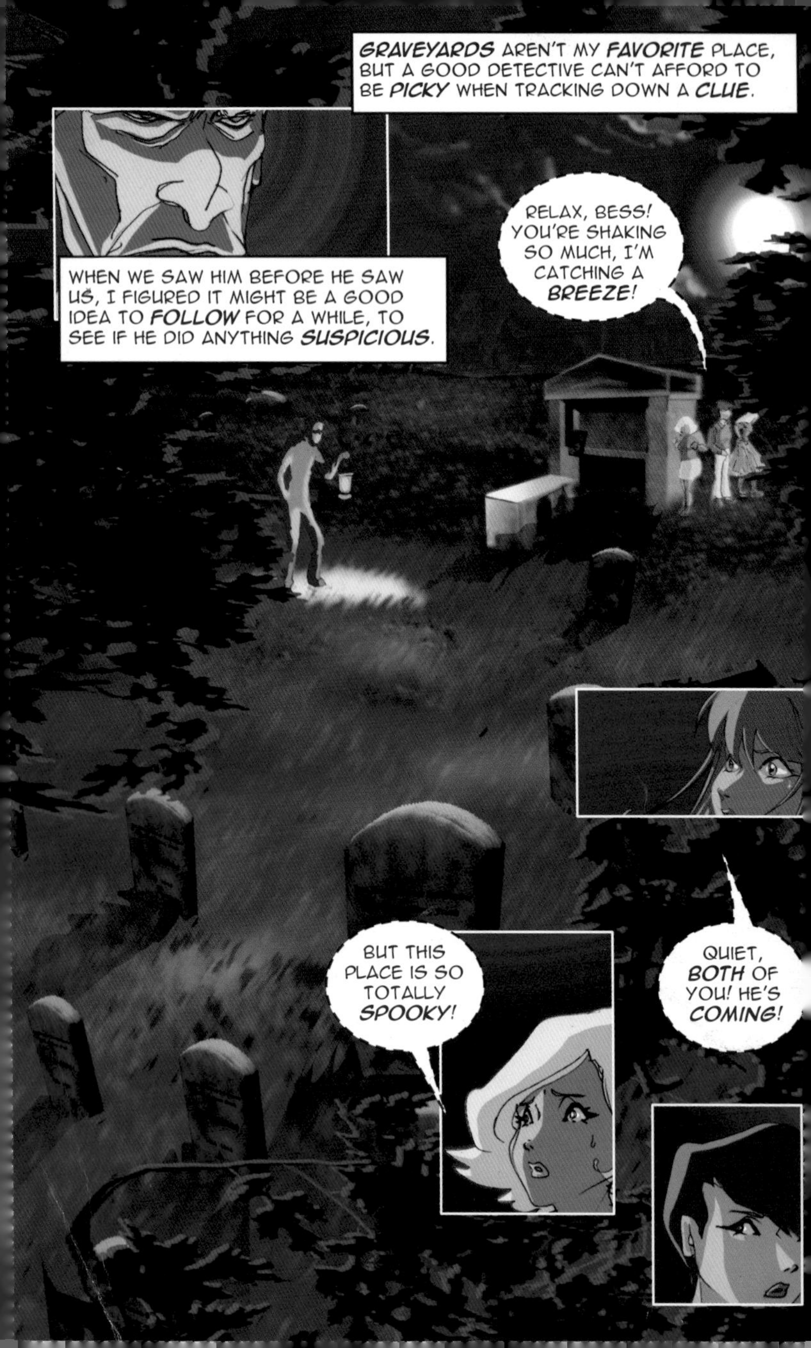
GRAVEYARDS AREN'T MY FAVORITE PLACE, BUT A GOOD DETECTIVE CAN'T AFFORD TO BE PICKY WHEN TRACKING DOWN A CLUE.
WHEN WE SAW HIM BEFORE HE SAW US, I FIGURED IT MIGHT BE A GOOD IDEA TO FOLLOW FOR A WHILE, TO SEE IF HE DID ANYTHING SUSPICIOUS.
RELAX, BESS! YOU'RE SHAKING SO MUCH, I'M CATCHING A BREEZE!
BUT THIS PLACE IS SO TOTALLY SPOOKY!
QUIET, BOTH OF YOU! HE'S COMING!

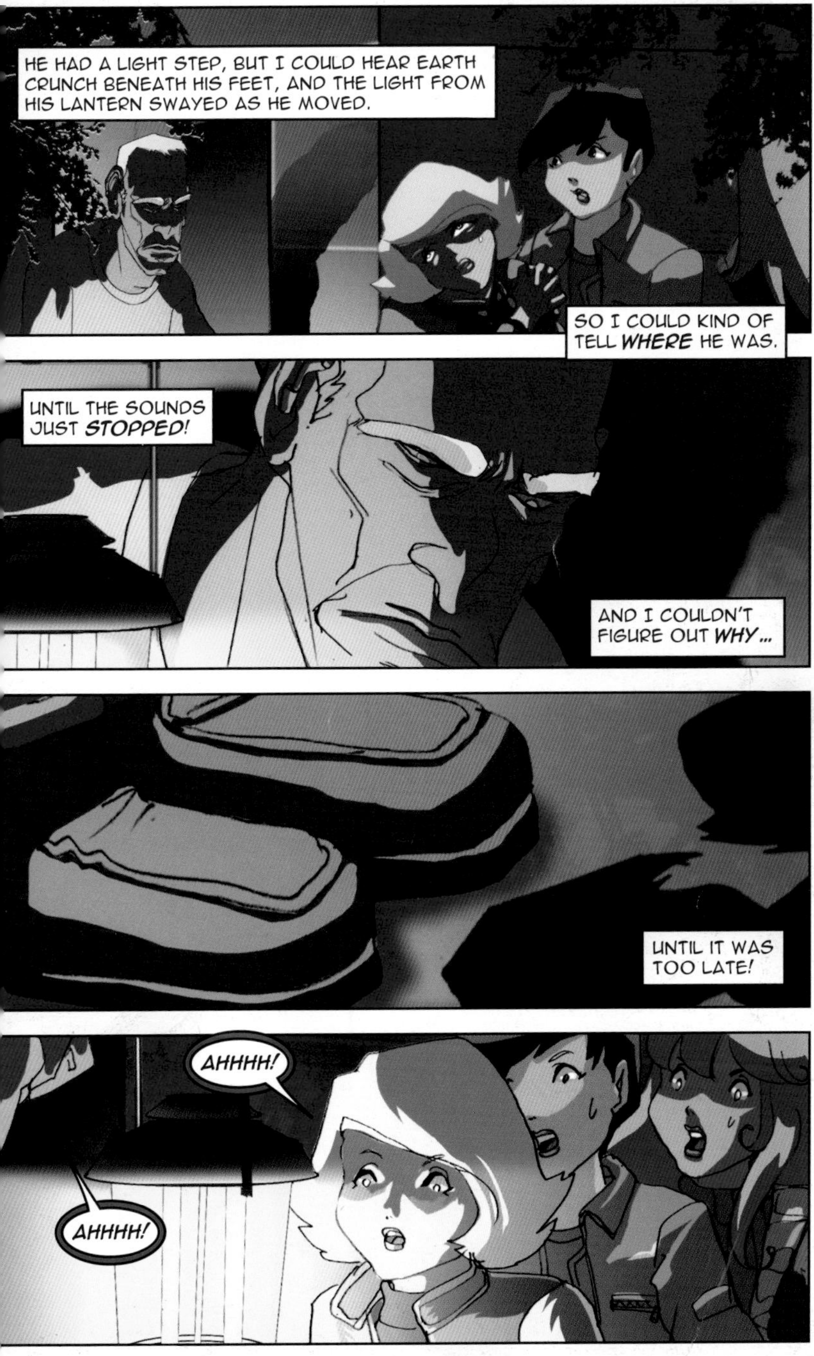
HE HAD A LIGHT STEP, BUT I COULD HEAR EARTH CRUNCH BENEATH HIS FEET, AND THE LIGHT FROM HIS LANTERN SWAYED AS HE MOVED.
SO I COULD KIND OF TELL *WHERE* HE WAS.
UNTIL THE SOUNDS JUST *STOPPED!*
AND I COULDN'T FIGURE OUT *WHY...*
UNTIL IT WAS TOO LATE!
AHHHH!
AHHHH!

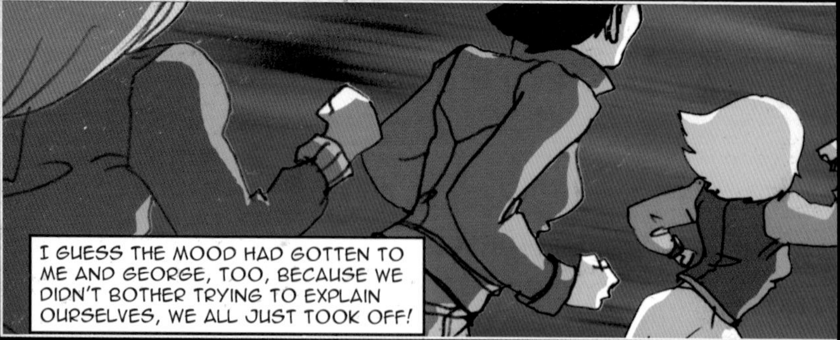
I GUESS THE MOOD HAD GOTTEN TO ME AND GEORGE, TOO, BECAUSE WE DIDN'T BOTHER TRYING TO EXPLAIN OURSELVES, WE ALL JUST TOOK OFF!

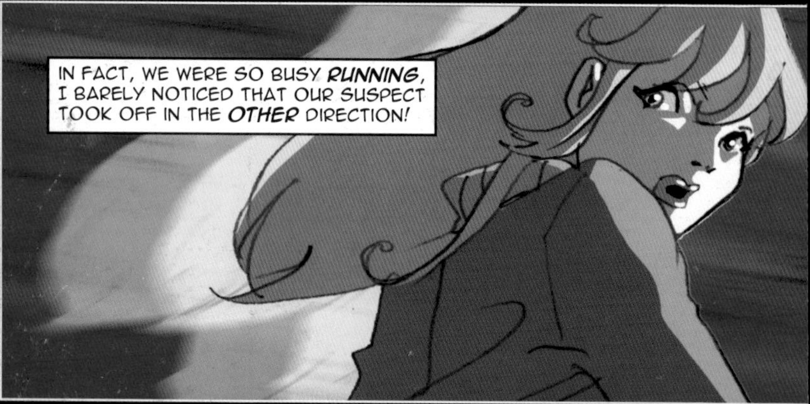
IN FACT, WE WERE SO BUSY *RUNNING*, I BARELY NOTICED THAT OUR SUSPECT TOOK OFF IN THE *OTHER* DIRECTION!

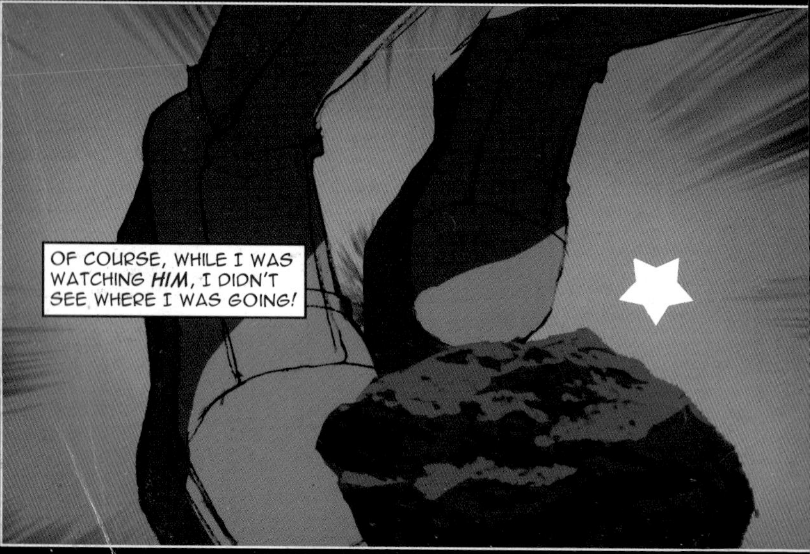
OF COURSE, WHILE I WAS WATCHING *HIM*, I DIDN'T SEE WHERE I WAS GOING!

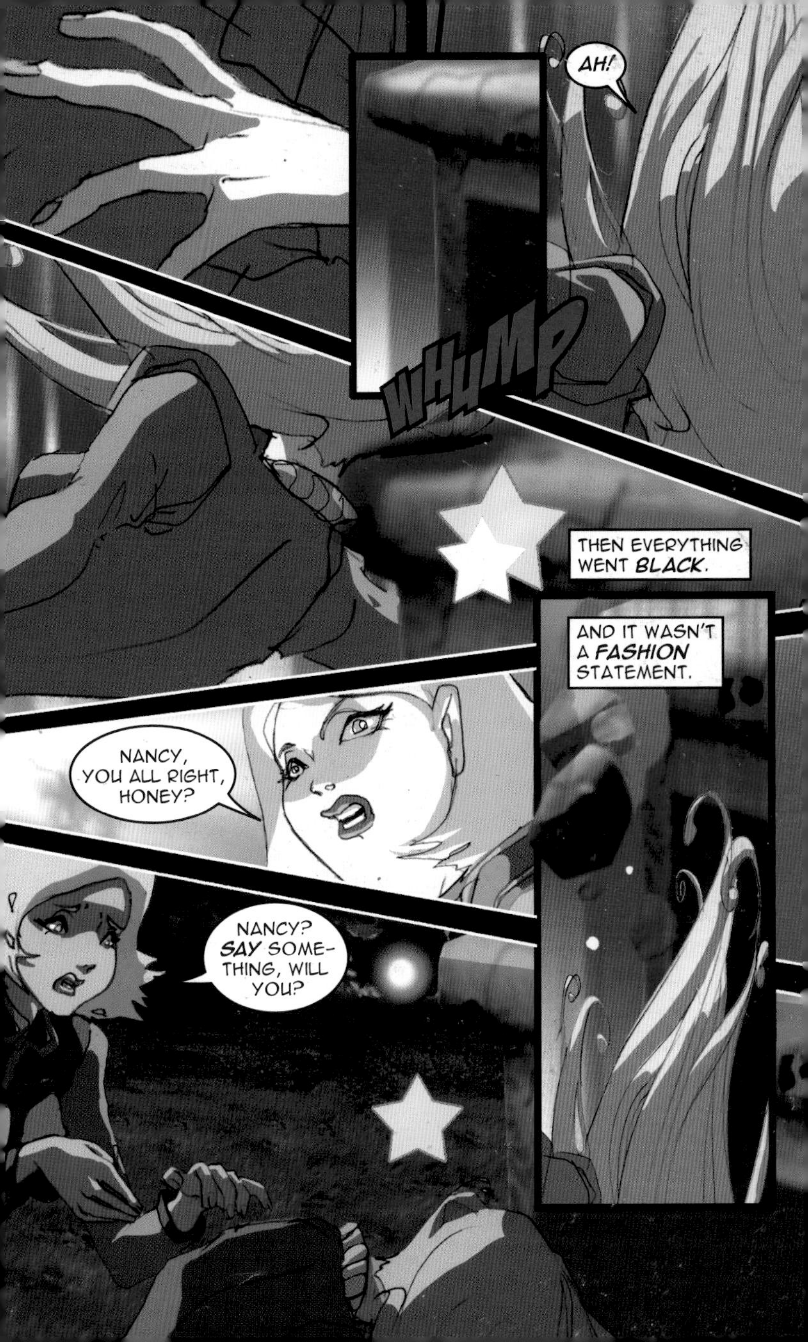
AH!
WHUMP
THEN EVERYTHING WENT BLACK.
AND IT WASN'T A FASHION STATEMENT.
NANCY, YOU ALL RIGHT, HONEY?
NANCY? SAY SOMETHING, WILL YOU?

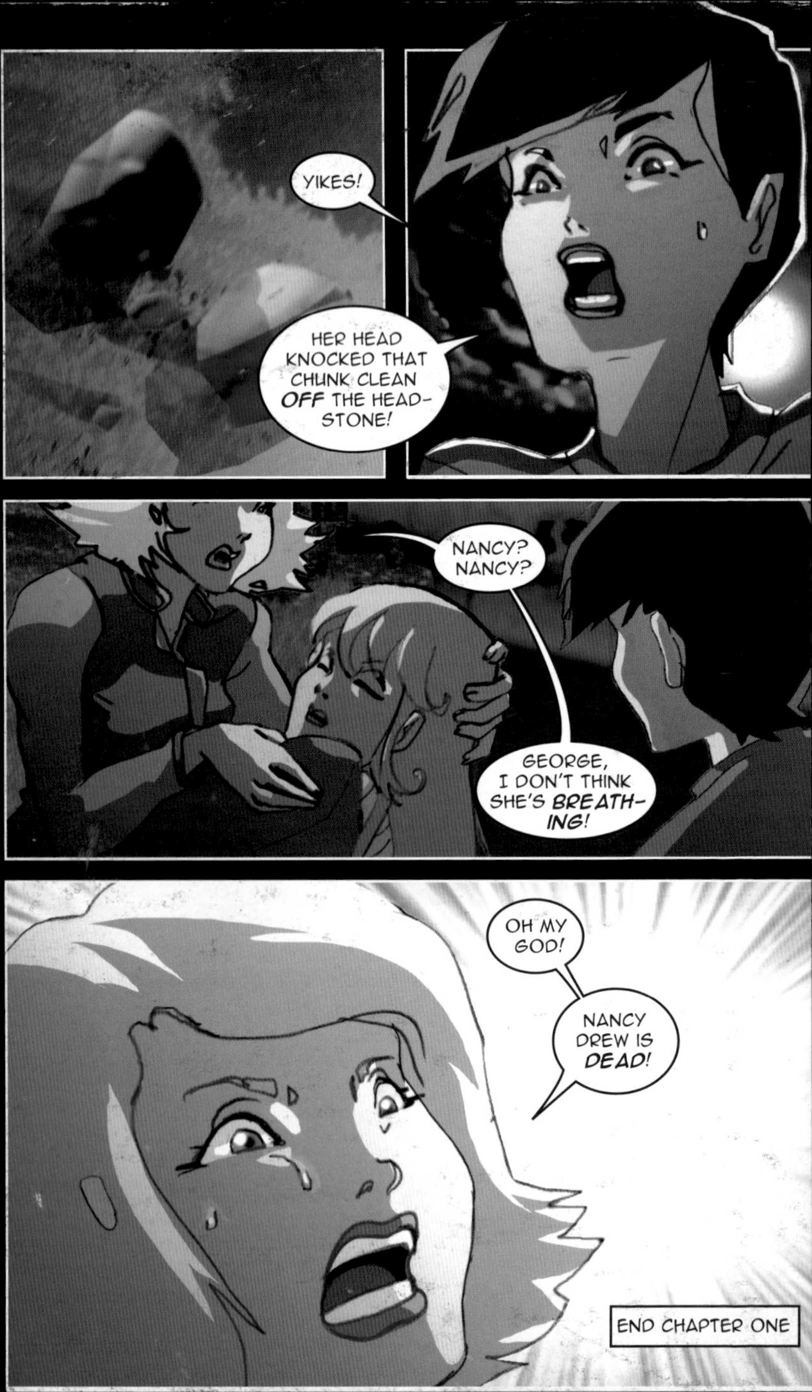
YIKES!
HER HEAD KNOCKED THAT CHUNK CLEAN OFF THE HEAD-STONE!
NANCY? NANCY?
GEORGE, I DON'T THINK SHE'S BREATH-ING!
OH MY GOD!
NANCY DREW IS DEAD!
END CHAPTER ONE

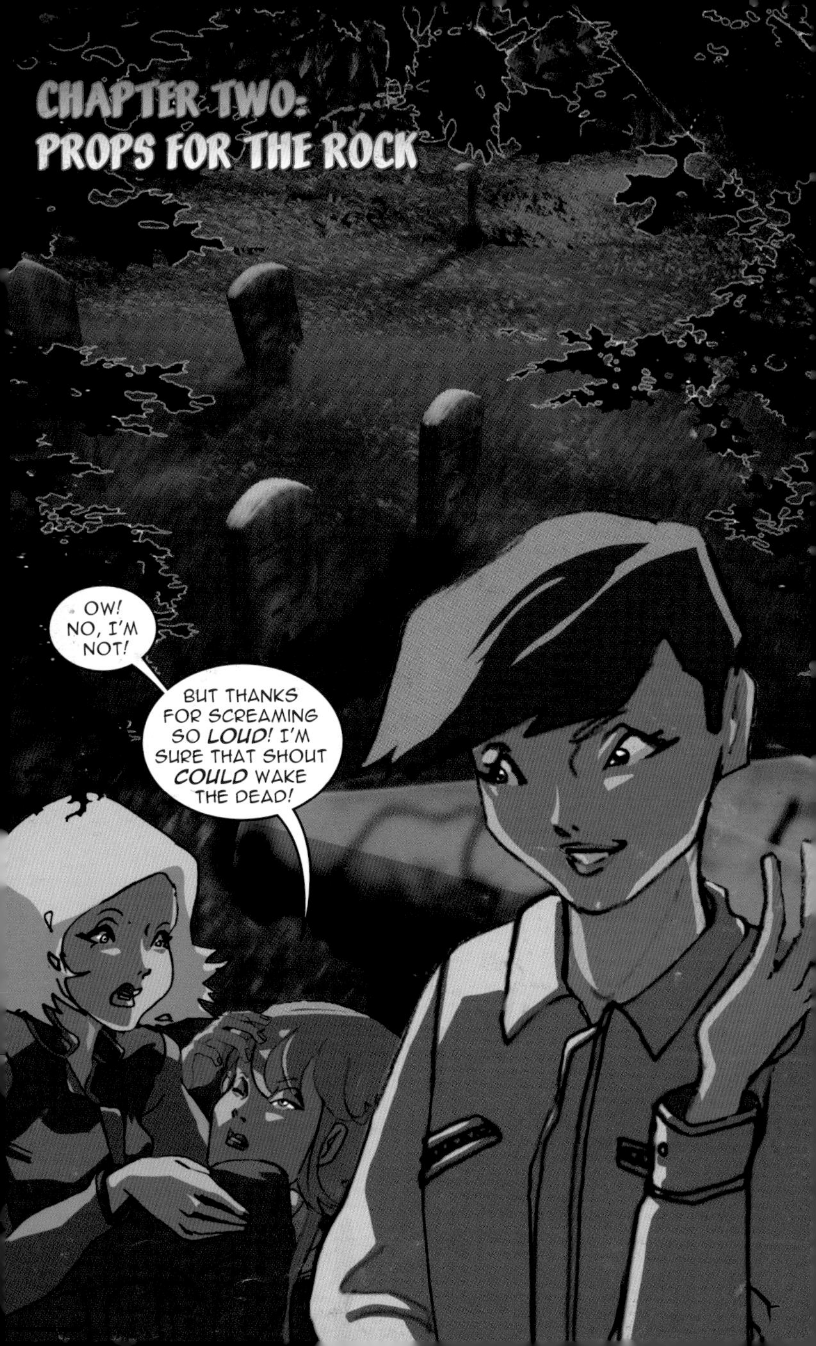
CHAPTER TWO:
PROPS FOR THE ROCK
OW! NO, I'M NOT!
BUT THANKS FOR SCREAMING SO LOUD! I'M SURE THAT SHOUT COULD WAKE THE DEAD!

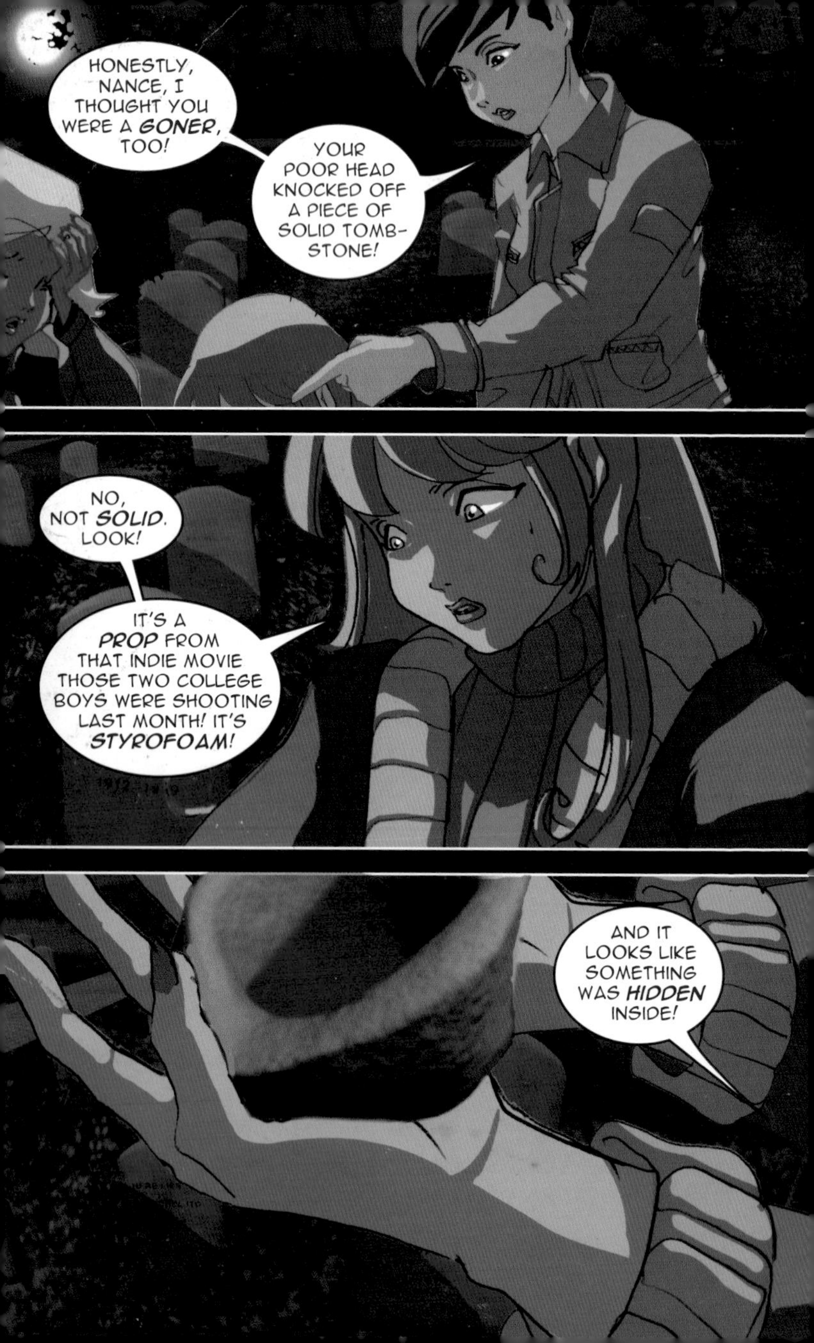

HONESTLY, NANCE, I THOUGHT YOU WERE A *GONER*, TOO!
YOUR POOR HEAD KNOCKED OFF A PIECE OF SOLID TOMB-STONE!
NO, NOT *SOLID*. LOOK!
IT'S A *PROP* FROM THAT INDIE MOVIE THOSE TWO COLLEGE BOYS WERE SHOOTING LAST MONTH! IT'S *STYROFOAM*!
AND IT LOOKS LIKE SOMETHING WAS *HIDDEN* INSIDE!

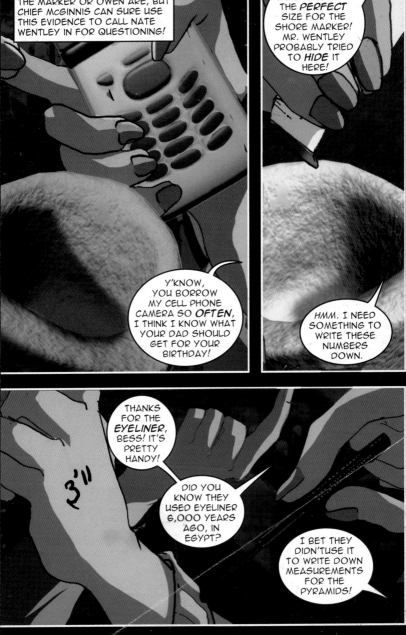

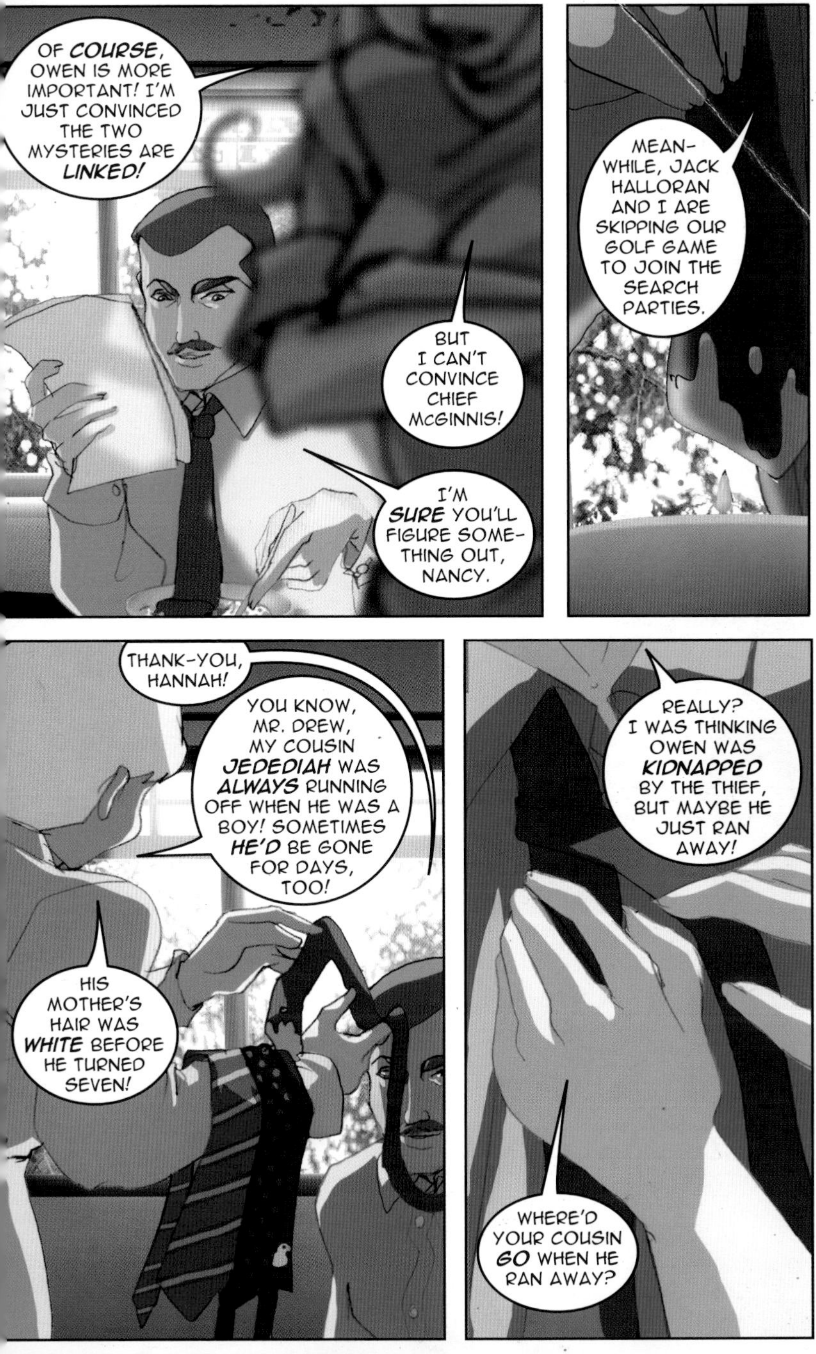

OF COURSE, OWEN IS MORE IMPORTANT! I'M JUST CONVINCED THE TWO MYSTERIES ARE LINKED!
BUT I CAN'T CONVINCE CHIEF MCGINNIS!
I'M SURE YOU'LL FIGURE SOME-THING OUT, NANCY.
MEAN-WHILE, JACK HALLORAN AND I ARE SKIPPING OUR GOLF GAME TO JOIN THE SEARCH PARTIES.
THANK-YOU, HANNAH!
YOU KNOW, MR. DREW, MY COUSIN JEDEDIAH WAS ALWAYS RUNNING OFF WHEN HE WAS A BOY! SOMETIMES HE'D BE GONE FOR DAYS, TOO!
HIS MOTHER'S HAIR WAS WHITE BEFORE HE TURNED SEVEN!
REALLY? I WAS THINKING OWEN WAS KIDNAPPED BY THE THIEF, BUT MAYBE HE JUST RAN AWAY!
WHERE'D YOUR COUSIN GO WHEN HE RAN AWAY?

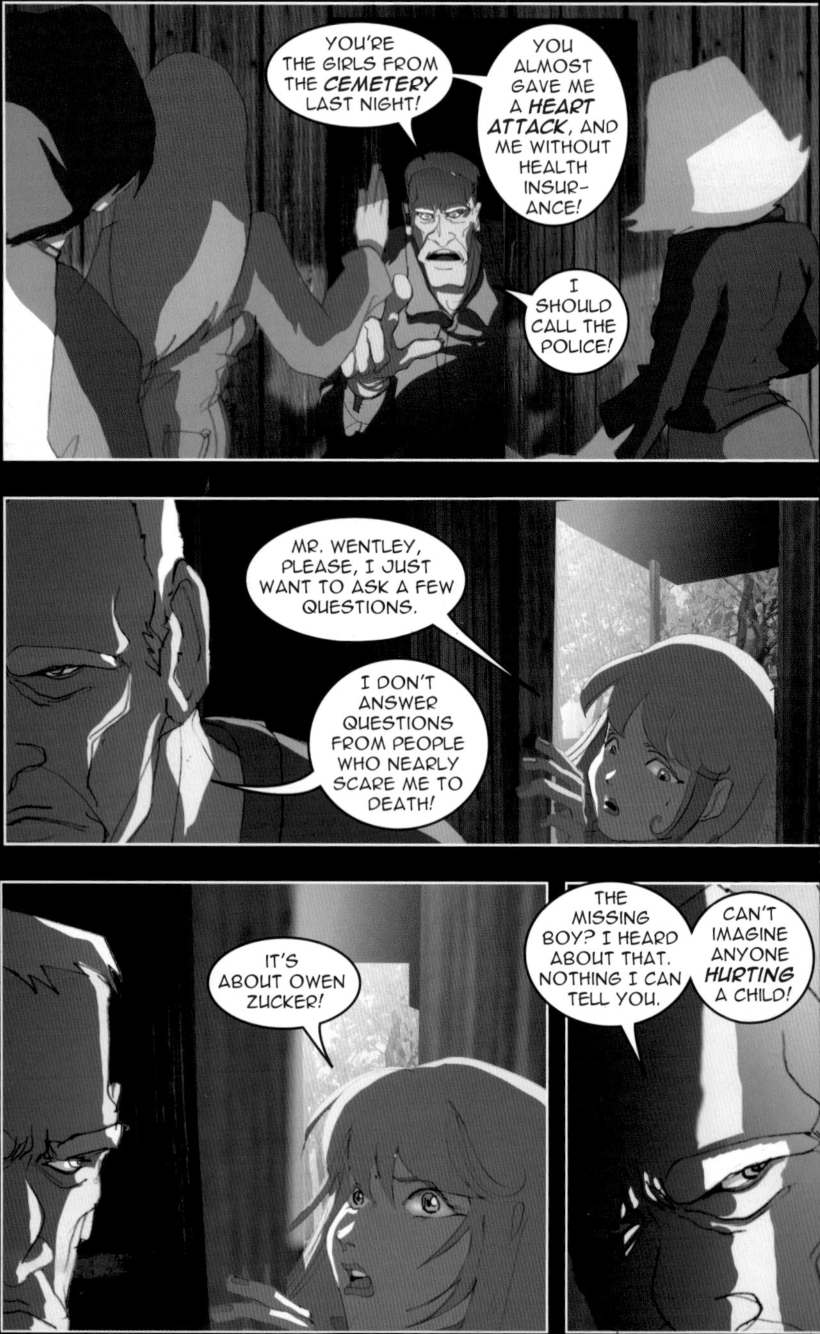
YOU'RE THE GIRLS FROM THE CEMETERY LAST NIGHT!
YOU ALMOST GAVE ME A HEART ATTACK, AND ME WITHOUT HEALTH INSURANCE!
I SHOULD CALL THE POLICE!
MR. WENTLEY, PLEASE, I JUST WANT TO ASK A FEW QUESTIONS.
I DON'T ANSWER QUESTIONS FROM PEOPLE WHO NEARLY SCARE ME TO DEATH!
IT'S ABOUT OWEN ZUCKER!
THE MISSING BOY? I HEARD ABOUT THAT. NOTHING I CAN TELL YOU.
CAN'T IMAGINE ANYONE HURTING A CHILD!

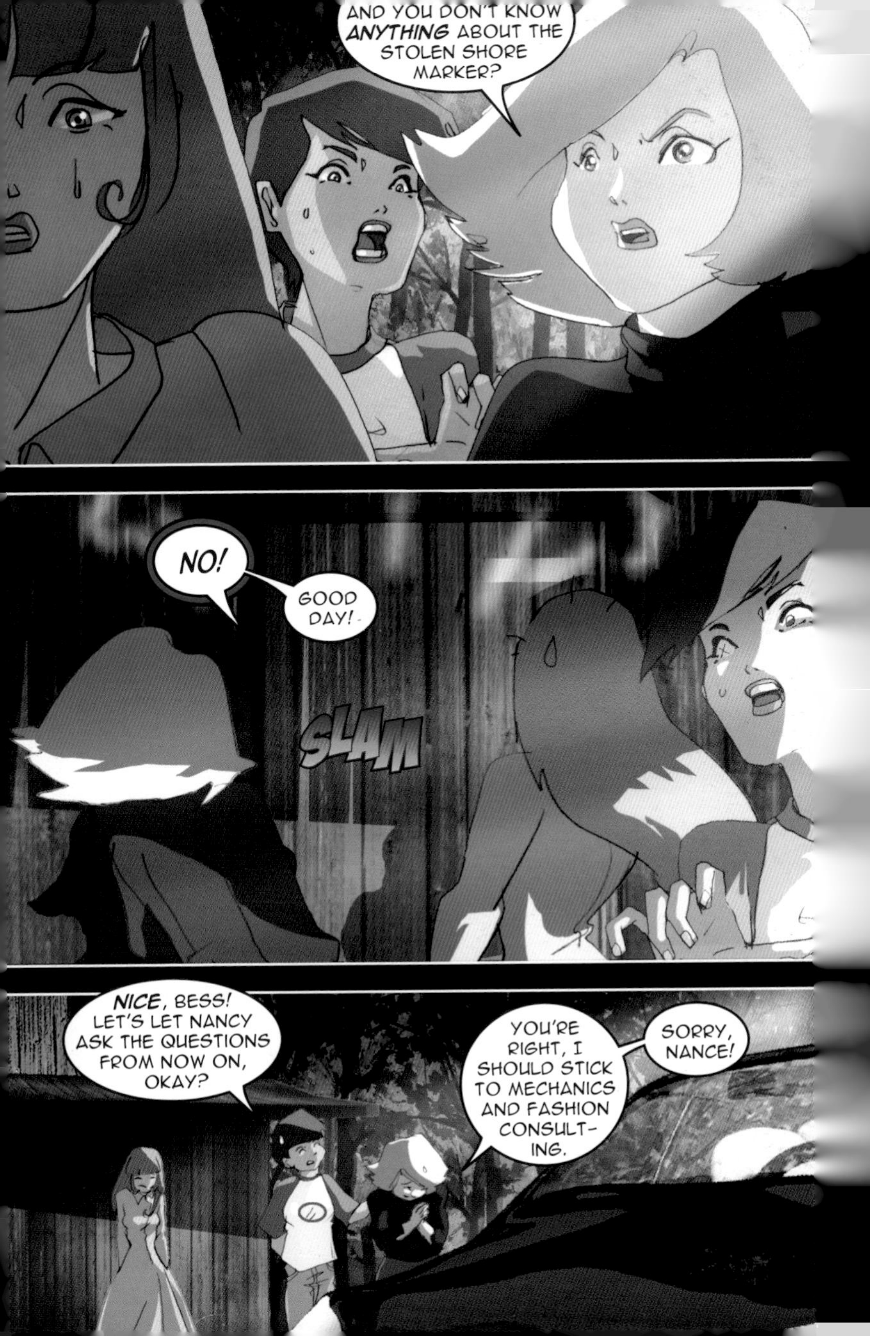
AND YOU DON'T KNOW ANYTHING ABOUT THE STOLEN SHORE MARKER?
NO!
GOOD DAY!
SLAM
NICE, BESS! LET'S LET NANCY ASK THE QUESTIONS FROM NOW ON, OKAY?
YOU'RE RIGHT, I SHOULD STICK TO MECHANICS AND FASHION CONSULT-ING.
SORRY, NANCE!

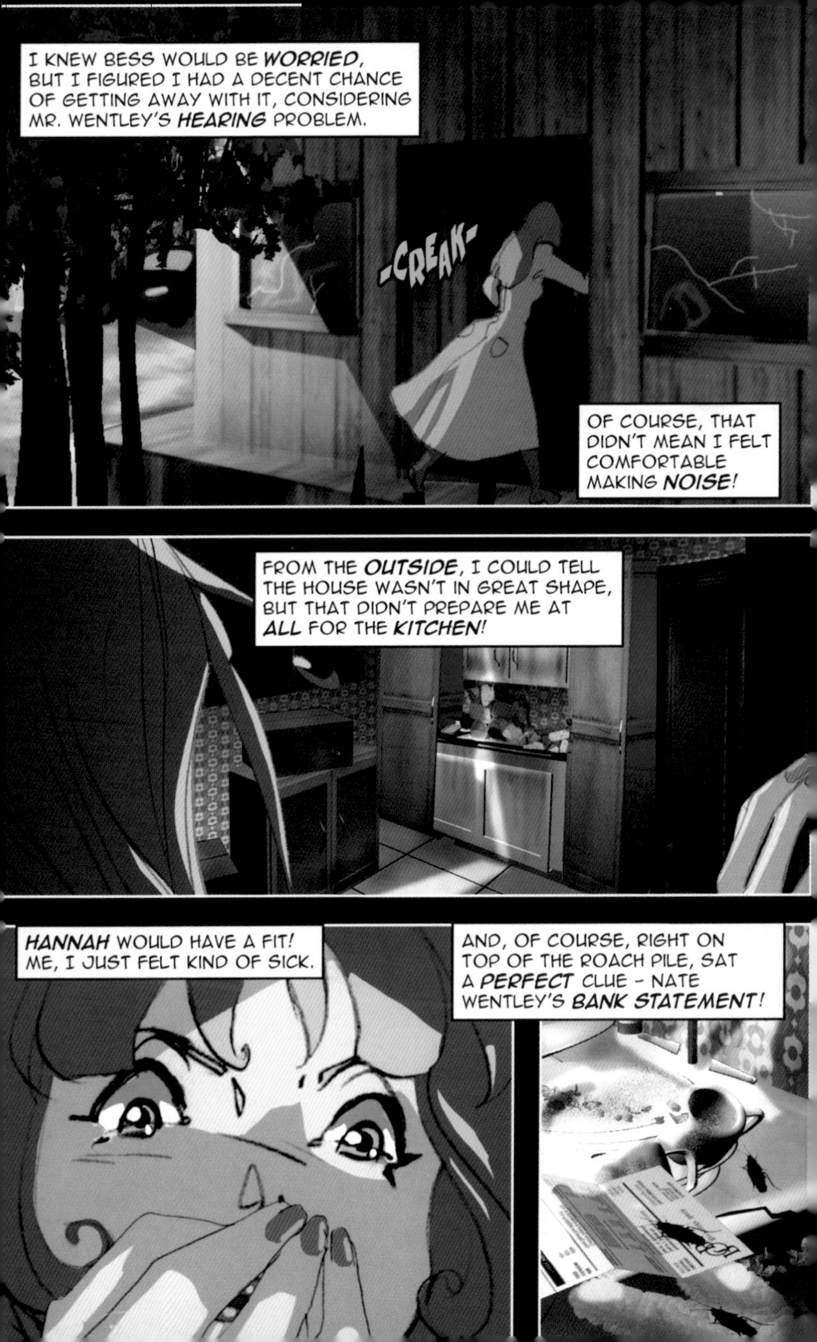
I KNEW BESS WOULD BE WORRIED, BUT I FIGURED I HAD A DECENT CHANCE OF GETTING AWAY WITH IT, CONSIDERING MR. WENTLEY'S HEARING PROBLEM.
-CREAK-
OF COURSE, THAT DIDN'T MEAN I FELT COMFORTABLE MAKING NOISE!
FROM THE OUTSIDE, I COULD TELL THE HOUSE WASN'T IN GREAT SHAPE, BUT THAT DIDN'T PREPARE ME AT ALL FOR THE KITCHEN!
HANNAH WOULD HAVE A FIT! ME, I JUST FELT KIND OF SICK.
AND, OF COURSE, RIGHT ON TOP OF THE ROACH PILE, SAT A PERFECT CLUE - NATE WENTLEY'S BANK STATEMENT!

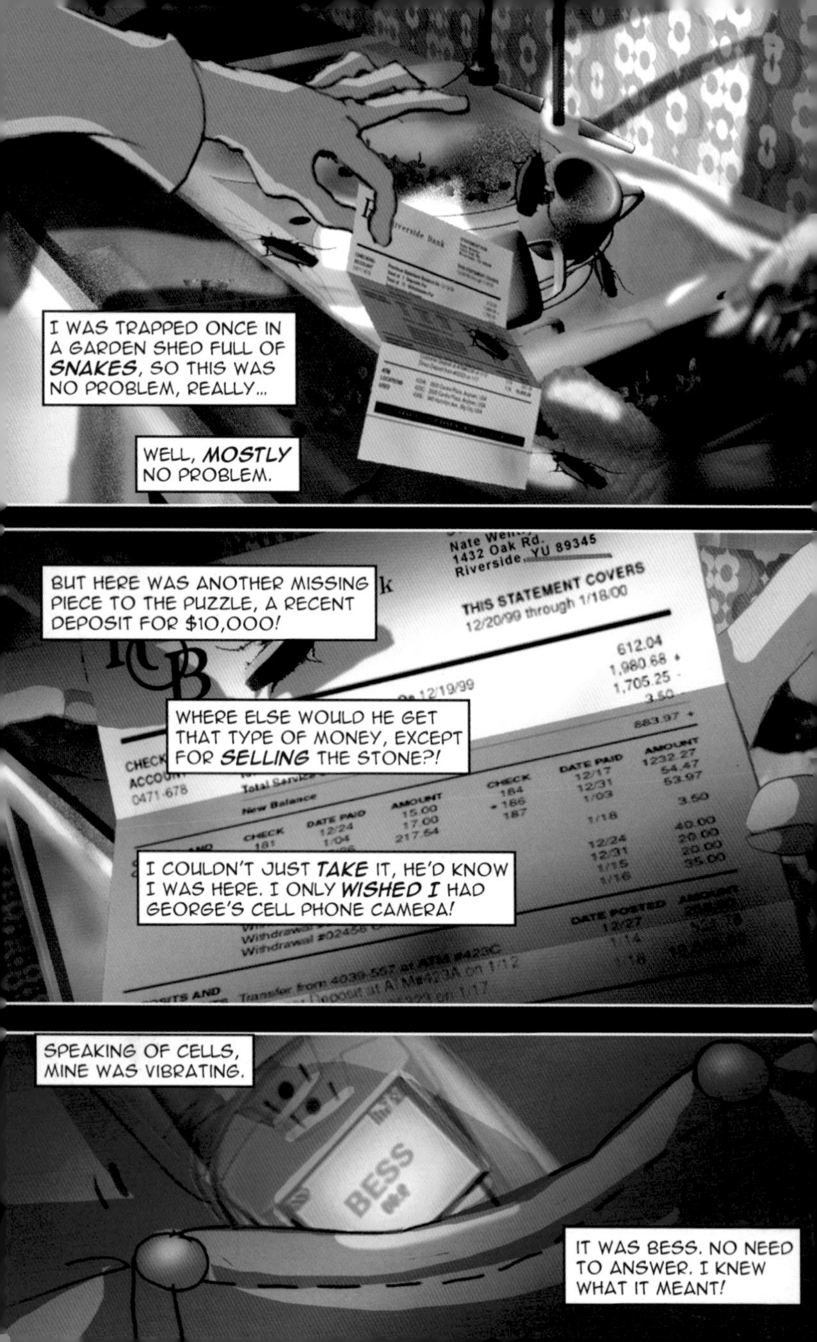
I WAS TRAPPED ONCE IN A GARDEN SHED FULL OF *SNAKES*, SO THIS WAS NO PROBLEM, REALLY...
WELL, *MOSTLY* NO PROBLEM.
BUT HERE WAS ANOTHER MISSING PIECE TO THE PUZZLE, A RECENT DEPOSIT FOR $10,000!
1432 Oak Rd.
Riverside, YU 89345
THIS STATEMENT COVERS
12/20/99 through 1/18/00
WHERE ELSE WOULD HE GET THAT TYPE OF MONEY, EXCEPT FOR *SELLING* THE STONE?!
I COULDN'T JUST *TAKE* IT, HE'D KNOW I WAS HERE. I ONLY *WISHED I* HAD GEORGE'S CELL PHONE CAMERA!
SPEAKING OF CELLS, MINE WAS VIBRATING.
BESS
IT WAS BESS. NO NEED TO ANSWER. I KNEW WHAT IT MEANT!

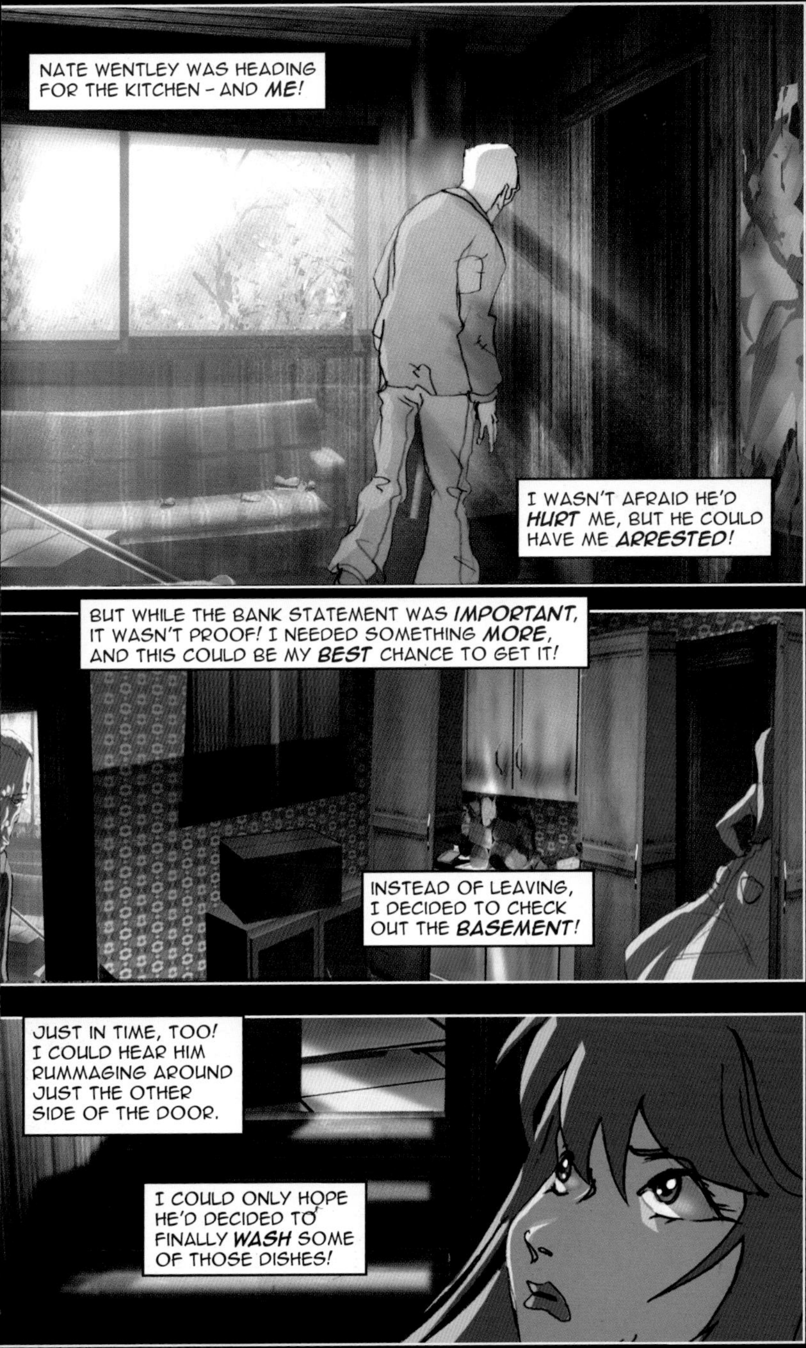
NATE WENTLEY WAS HEADING FOR THE KITCHEN - AND ME!
I WASN'T AFRAID HE'D HURT ME, BUT HE COULD HAVE ME ARRESTED!
BUT WHILE THE BANK STATEMENT WAS IMPORTANT, IT WASN'T PROOF! I NEEDED SOMETHING MORE, AND THIS COULD BE MY BEST CHANCE TO GET IT!
INSTEAD OF LEAVING, I DECIDED TO CHECK OUT THE BASEMENT!
JUST IN TIME, TOO! I COULD HEAR HIM RUMMAGING AROUND JUST THE OTHER SIDE OF THE DOOR.
I COULD ONLY HOPE HE'D DECIDED TO FINALLY WASH SOME OF THOSE DISHES!

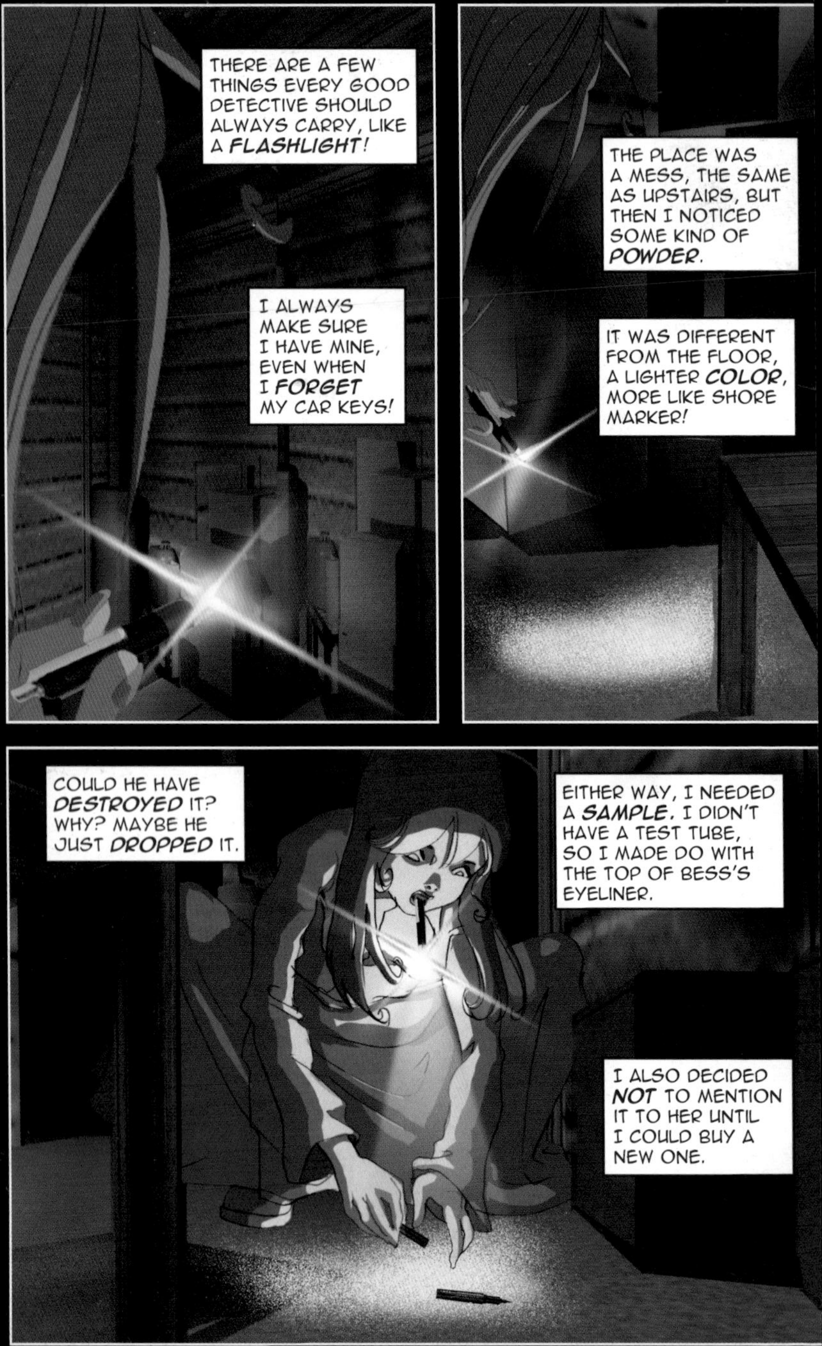
THERE ARE A FEW THINGS EVERY GOOD DETECTIVE SHOULD ALWAYS CARRY, LIKE A FLASHLIGHT!
I ALWAYS MAKE SURE I HAVE MINE, EVEN WHEN I FORGET MY CAR KEYS!
THE PLACE WAS A MESS, THE SAME AS UPSTAIRS, BUT THEN I NOTICED SOME KIND OF POWDER.
IT WAS DIFFERENT FROM THE FLOOR, A LIGHTER COLOR, MORE LIKE SHORE MARKER!
COULD HE HAVE DESTROYED IT? WHY? MAYBE HE JUST DROPPED IT.
EITHER WAY, I NEEDED A SAMPLE. I DIDN'T HAVE A TEST TUBE, SO I MADE DO WITH THE TOP OF BESS'S EYELINER.
I ALSO DECIDED NOT TO MENTION IT TO HER UNTIL I COULD BUY A NEW ONE.

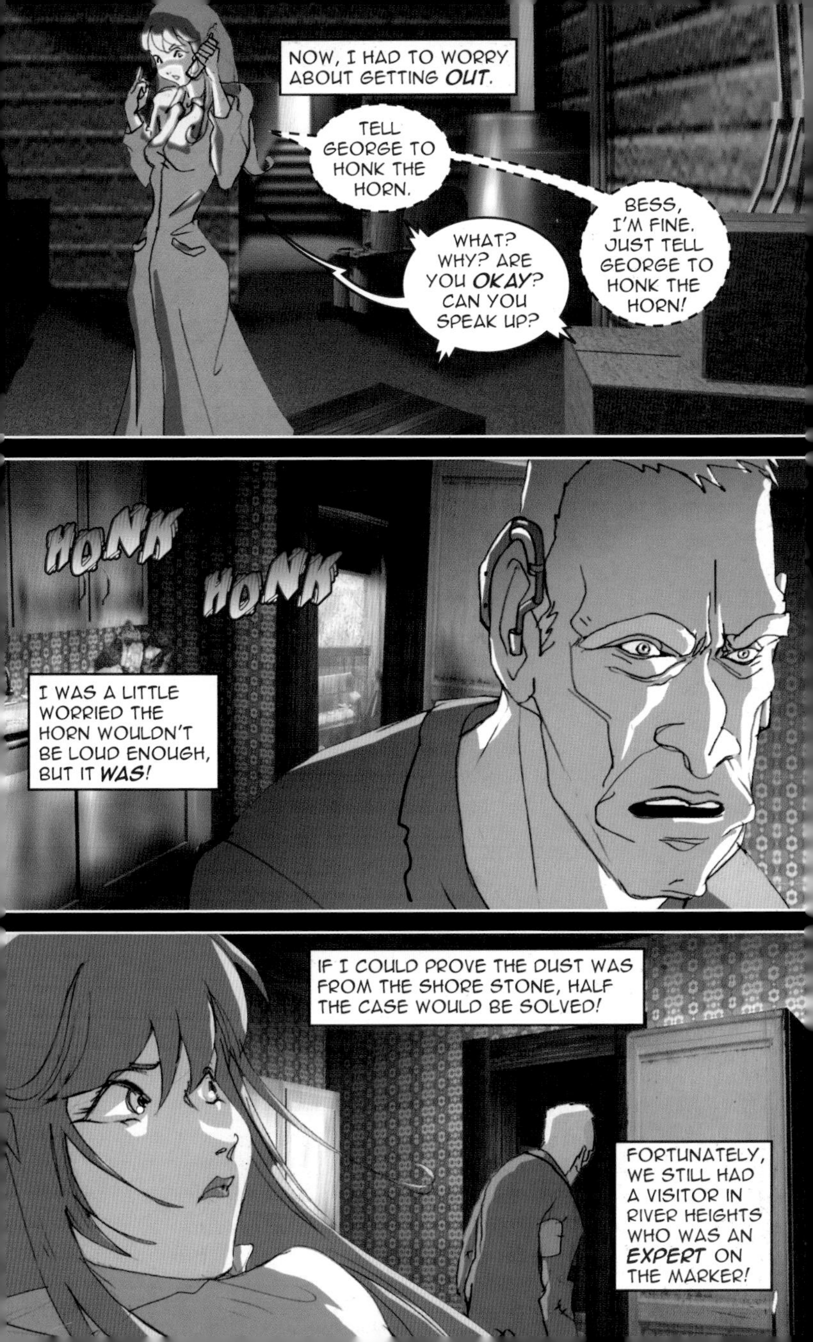

NOW, I HAD TO WORRY ABOUT GETTING OUT.
TELL GEORGE TO HONK THE HORN.
WHAT? WHY? ARE YOU OKAY? CAN YOU SPEAK UP?
BESS, I'M FINE. JUST TELL GEORGE TO HONK THE HORN!
HONK
HONK
I WAS A LITTLE WORRIED THE HORN WOULDN'T BE LOUD ENOUGH, BUT IT WAS!
IF I COULD PROVE THE DUST WAS FROM THE SHORE STONE, HALF THE CASE WOULD BE SOLVED!
FORTUNATELY, WE STILL HAD A VISITOR IN RIVER HEIGHTS WHO WAS AN EXPERT ON THE MARKER!

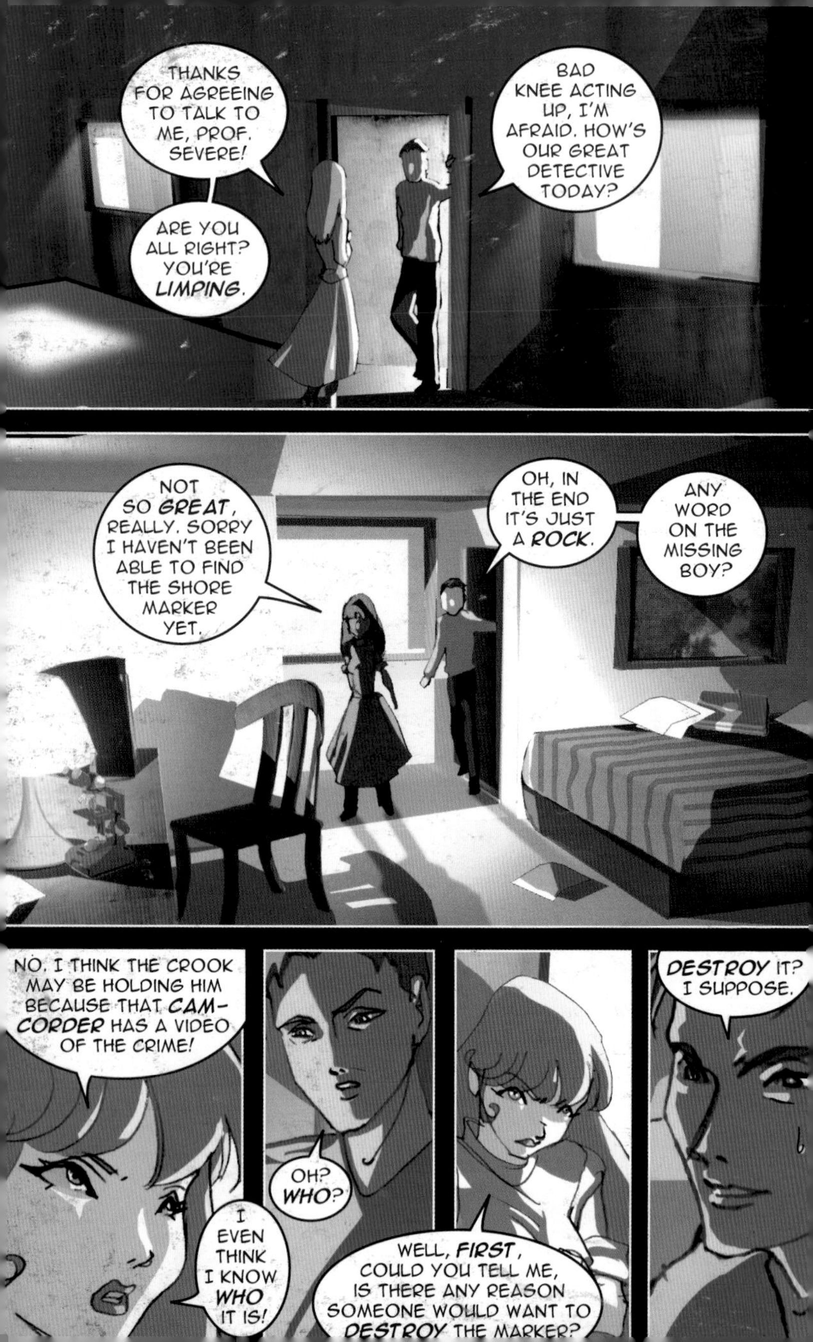
THANKS FOR AGREEING TO TALK TO ME, PROF. SEVERE!
ARE YOU ALL RIGHT? YOU'RE *LIMPING*.
BAD KNEE ACTING UP, I'M AFRAID. HOW'S OUR GREAT DETECTIVE TODAY?
NOT SO *GREAT*, REALLY. SORRY I HAVEN'T BEEN ABLE TO FIND THE SHORE MARKER YET.
OH, IN THE END IT'S JUST A *ROCK*.
ANY WORD ON THE MISSING BOY?
NO. I THINK THE CROOK MAY BE HOLDING HIM BECAUSE THAT *CAM-CORDER* HAS A VIDEO OF THE CRIME!
I EVEN THINK I KNOW *WHO* IT IS!
OH? *WHO*?
WELL, *FIRST*, COULD YOU TELL ME, IS THERE ANY REASON SOMEONE WOULD WANT TO *DESTROY* THE MARKER?
DESTROY IT? I SUPPOSE.

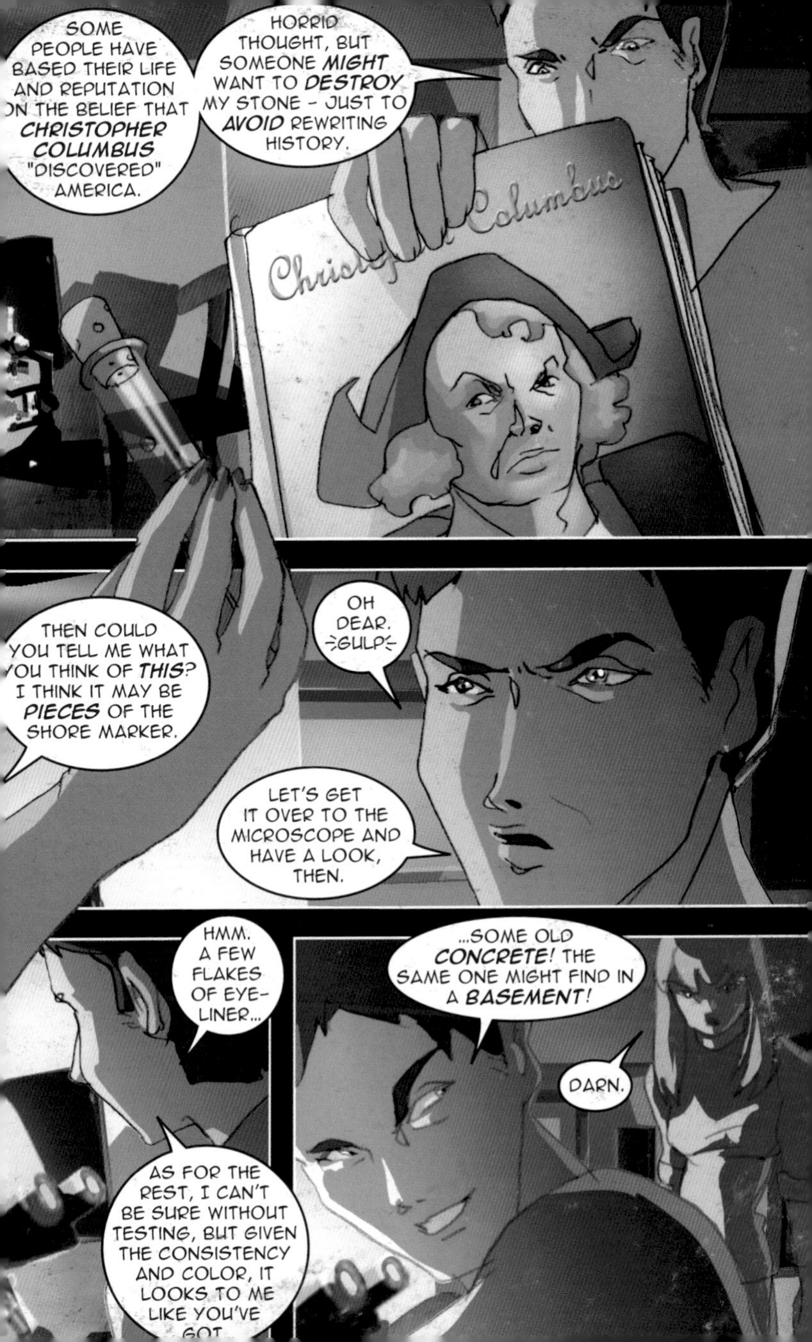
SOME PEOPLE HAVE BASED THEIR LIFE AND REPUTATION ON THE BELIEF THAT **CHRISTOPHER COLUMBUS** "DISCOVERED" AMERICA.
HORRID THOUGHT, BUT SOMEONE ***MIGHT*** WANT TO ***DESTROY*** MY STONE - JUST TO ***AVOID*** REWRITING HISTORY.
Christopher Columbus
THEN COULD YOU TELL ME WHAT YOU THINK OF ***THIS***? I THINK IT MAY BE ***PIECES*** OF THE SHORE MARKER.
OH DEAR. -GULP-
LET'S GET IT OVER TO THE MICROSCOPE AND HAVE A LOOK, THEN.
HMM. A FEW FLAKES OF EYE-LINER...
AS FOR THE REST, I CAN'T BE SURE WITHOUT TESTING, BUT GIVEN THE CONSISTENCY AND COLOR, IT LOOKS TO ME LIKE YOU'VE GOT
...SOME OLD ***CONCRETE!*** THE SAME ONE MIGHT FIND IN A ***BASEMENT!***
DARN.

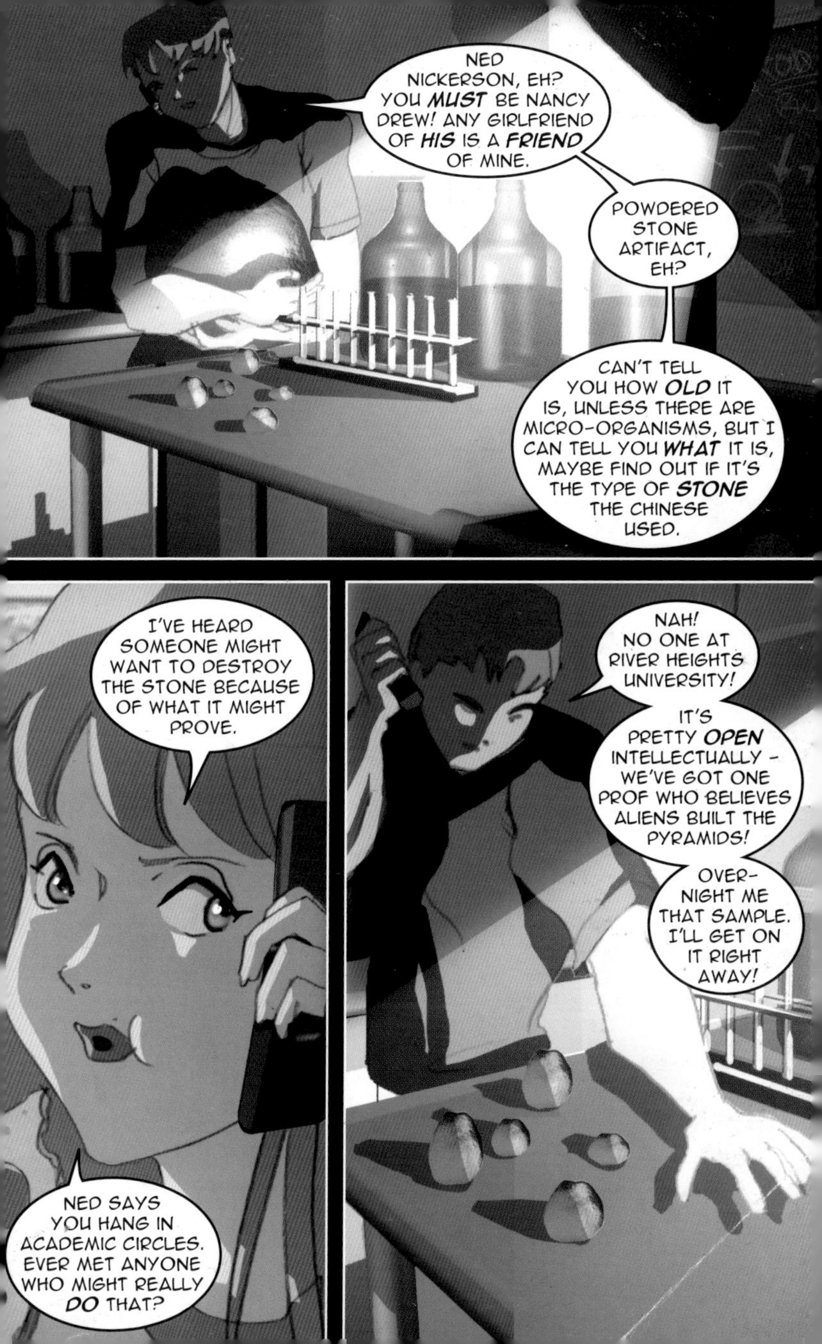
NED NICKERSON, EH? YOU MUST BE NANCY DREW! ANY GIRLFRIEND OF HIS IS A FRIEND OF MINE.
POWDERED STONE ARTIFACT, EH?
CAN'T TELL YOU HOW OLD IT IS, UNLESS THERE ARE MICRO-ORGANISMS, BUT I CAN TELL YOU WHAT IT IS, MAYBE FIND OUT IF IT'S THE TYPE OF STONE THE CHINESE USED.
I'VE HEARD SOMEONE MIGHT WANT TO DESTROY THE STONE BECAUSE OF WHAT IT MIGHT PROVE.
NED SAYS YOU HANG IN ACADEMIC CIRCLES. EVER MET ANYONE WHO MIGHT REALLY DO THAT?
NAH! NO ONE AT RIVER HEIGHTS UNIVERSITY!
IT'S PRETTY OPEN INTELLECTUALLY - WE'VE GOT ONE PROF WHO BELIEVES ALIENS BUILT THE PYRAMIDS!
OVER-NIGHT ME THAT SAMPLE. I'LL GET ON IT RIGHT AWAY!

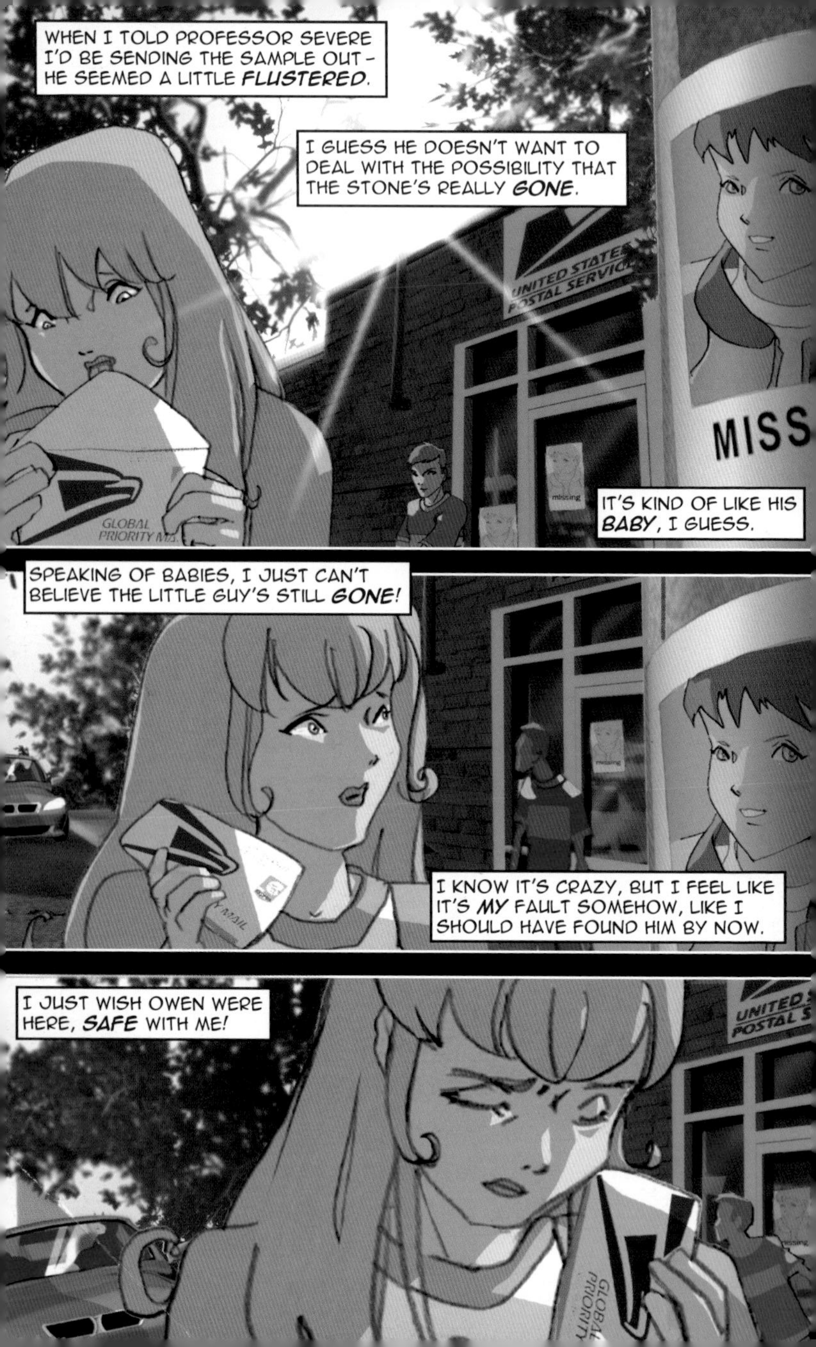
WHEN I TOLD PROFESSOR SEVERE I'D BE SENDING THE SAMPLE OUT - HE SEEMED A LITTLE FLUSTERED.
I GUESS HE DOESN'T WANT TO DEAL WITH THE POSSIBILITY THAT THE STONE'S REALLY GONE.
UNITED STATES POSTAL SERVICE
MISS
GLOBAL PRIORITY MA
missing
IT'S KIND OF LIKE HIS BABY, I GUESS.
SPEAKING OF BABIES, I JUST CAN'T BELIEVE THE LITTLE GUY'S STILL GONE!
I KNOW IT'S CRAZY, BUT I FEEL LIKE IT'S MY FAULT SOMEHOW, LIKE I SHOULD HAVE FOUND HIM BY NOW.
I JUST WISH OWEN WERE HERE, SAFE WITH ME!

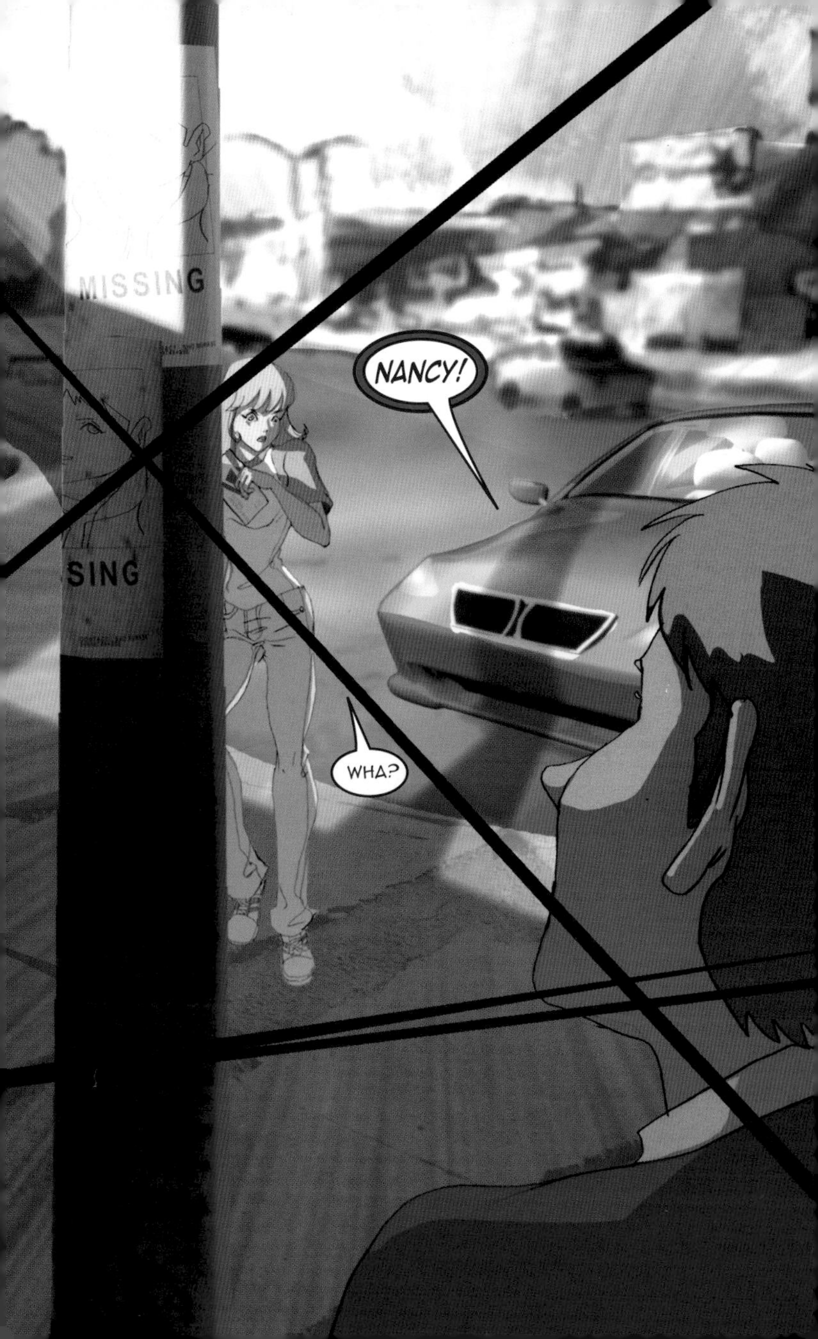
MISSING
SING
NANCY!
WHA?

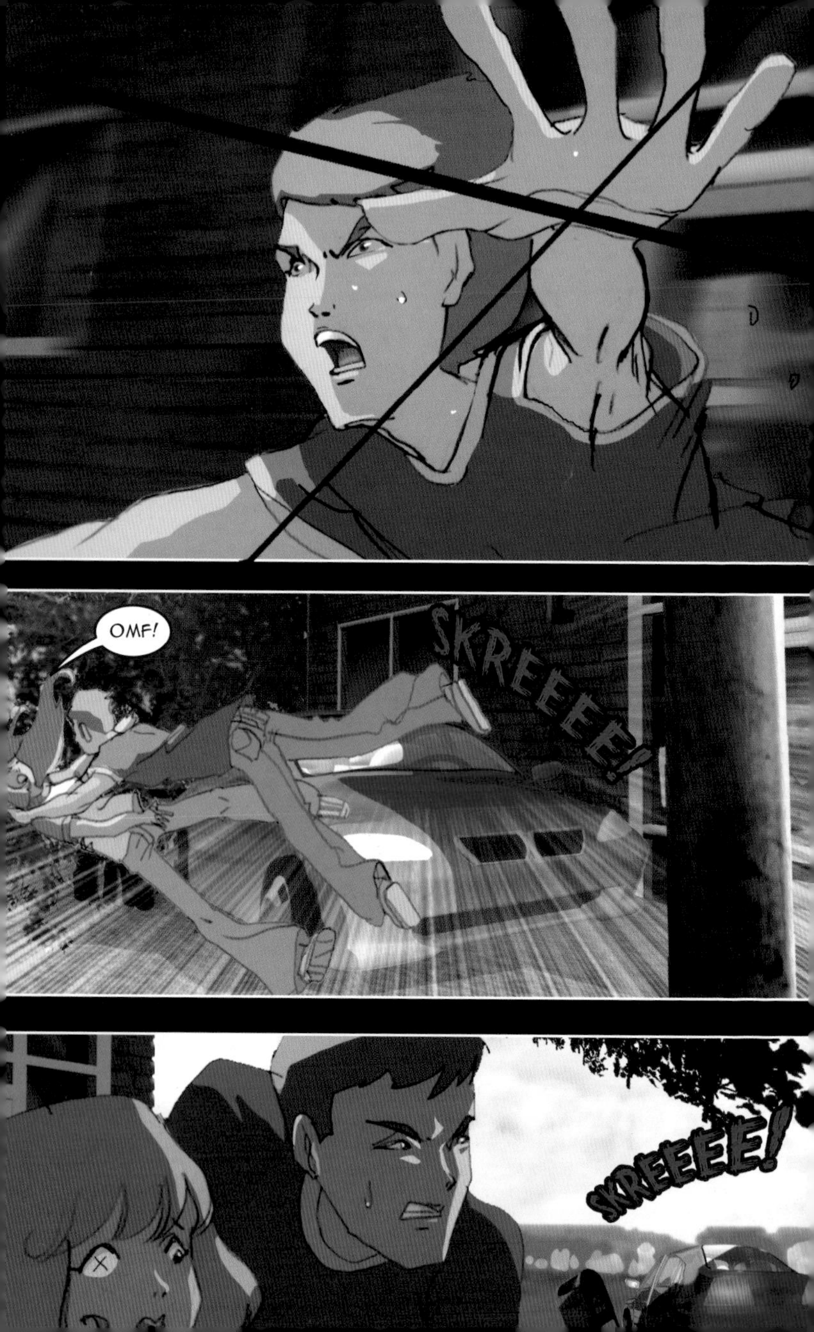

OMF!
SKREEEEE!
SKREEEEE!

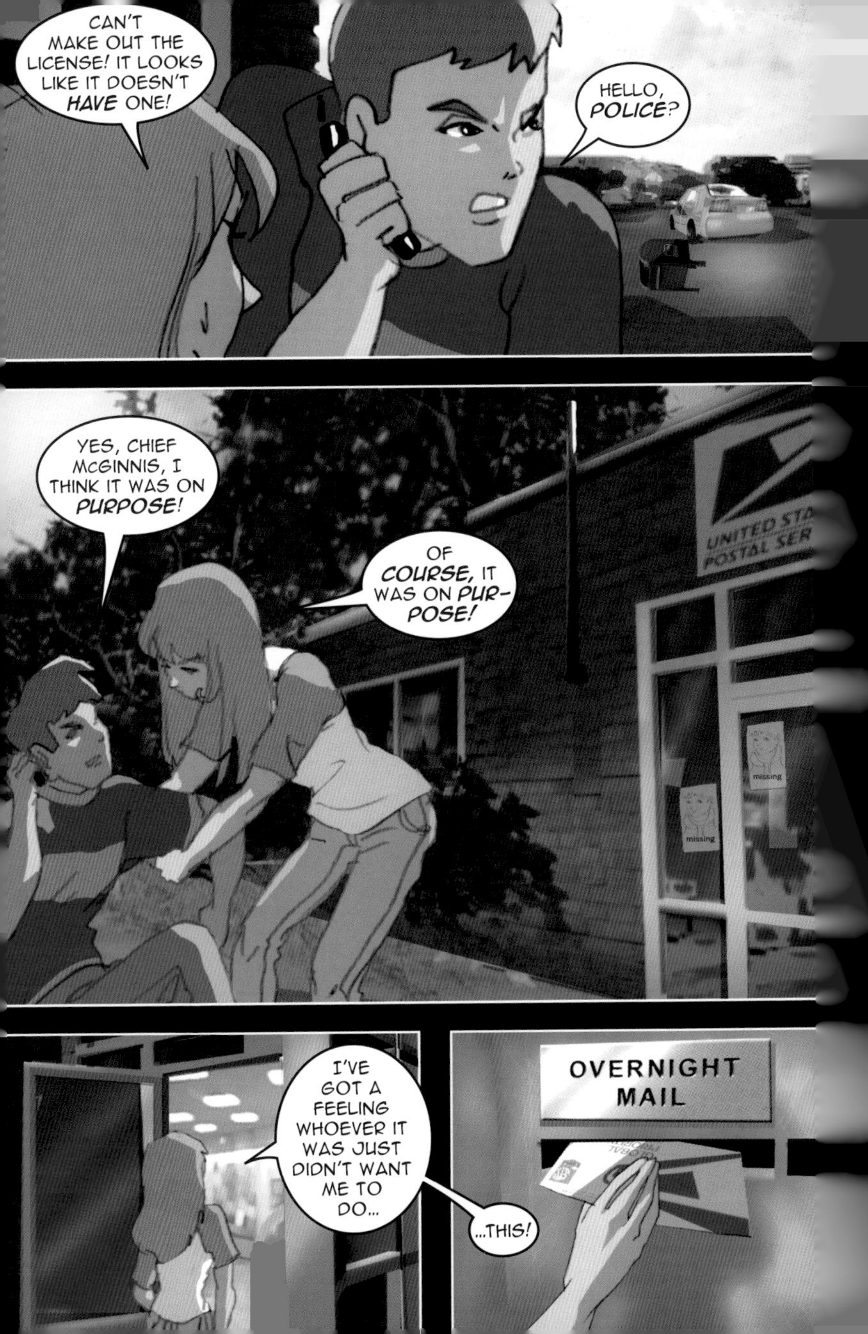
CAN'T MAKE OUT THE LICENSE! IT LOOKS LIKE IT DOESN'T HAVE ONE!
HELLO, POLICE?
YES, CHIEF McGINNIS, I THINK IT WAS ON PURPOSE!
OF COURSE, IT WAS ON PUR-POSE!
UNITED STA
POSTAL SER
missing
missing
I'VE GOT A FEELING WHOEVER IT WAS JUST DIDN'T WANT ME TO DO...
...THIS!
OVERNIGHT MAIL

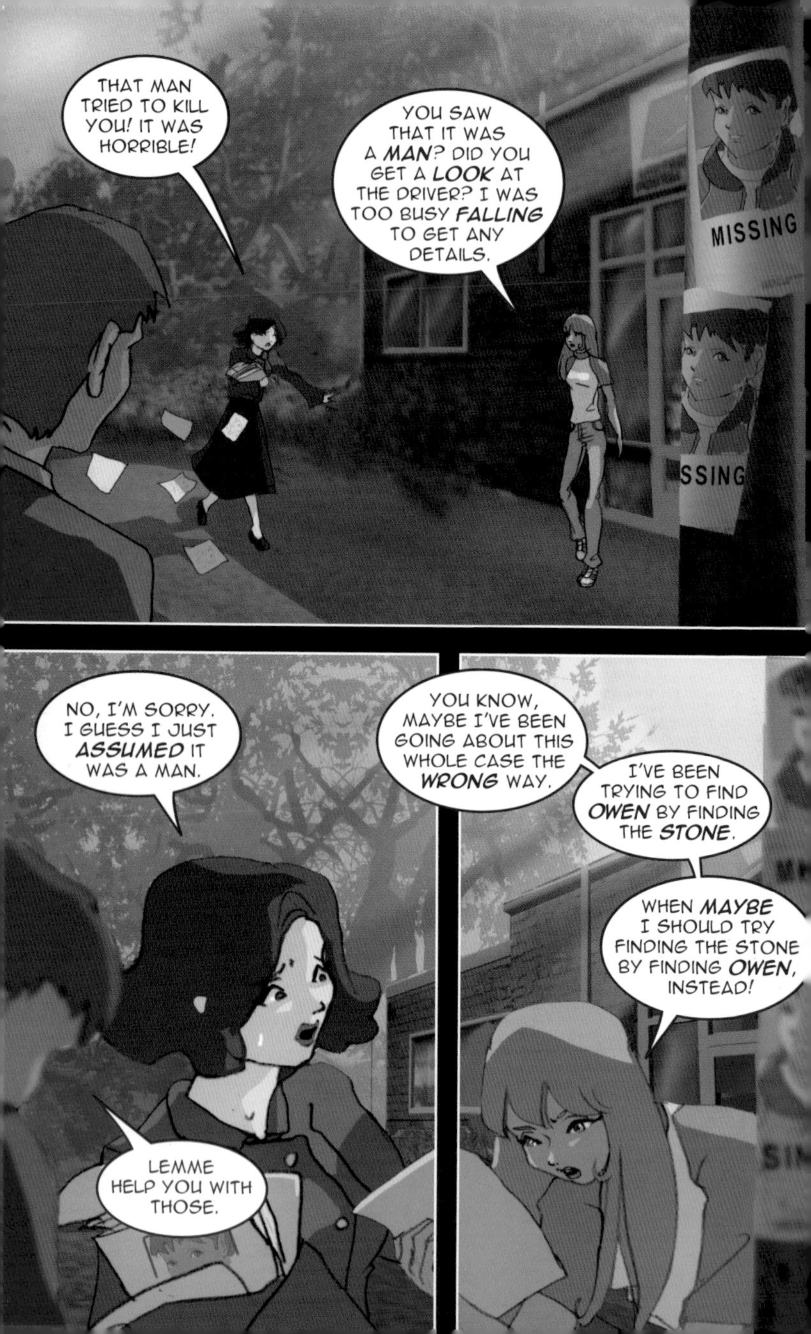
THAT MAN TRIED TO KILL YOU! IT WAS HORRIBLE!
YOU SAW THAT IT WAS A MAN? DID YOU GET A LOOK AT THE DRIVER? I WAS TOO BUSY FALLING TO GET ANY DETAILS.
MISSING
SSING
NO, I'M SORRY. I GUESS I JUST ASSUMED IT WAS A MAN.
LEMME HELP YOU WITH THOSE.
YOU KNOW, MAYBE I'VE BEEN GOING ABOUT THIS WHOLE CASE THE WRONG WAY.
I'VE BEEN TRYING TO FIND OWEN BY FINDING THE STONE.
WHEN MAYBE I SHOULD TRY FINDING THE STONE BY FINDING OWEN, INSTEAD!

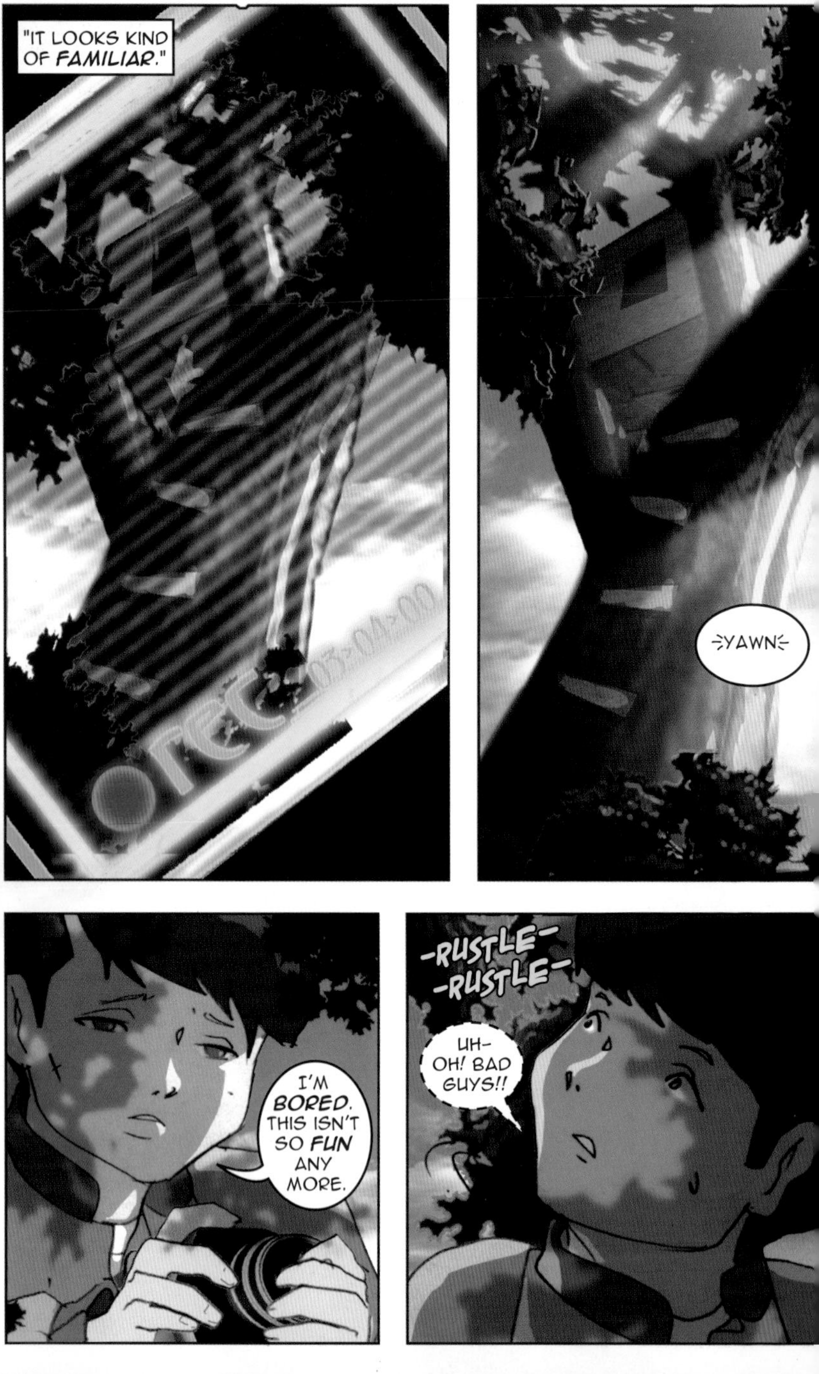
"IT LOOKS KIND OF FAMILIAR."
YAWN
I'M BORED. THIS ISN'T SO FUN ANY MORE.
-RUSTLE-
-RUSTLE-
UH-OH! BAD GUYS!!

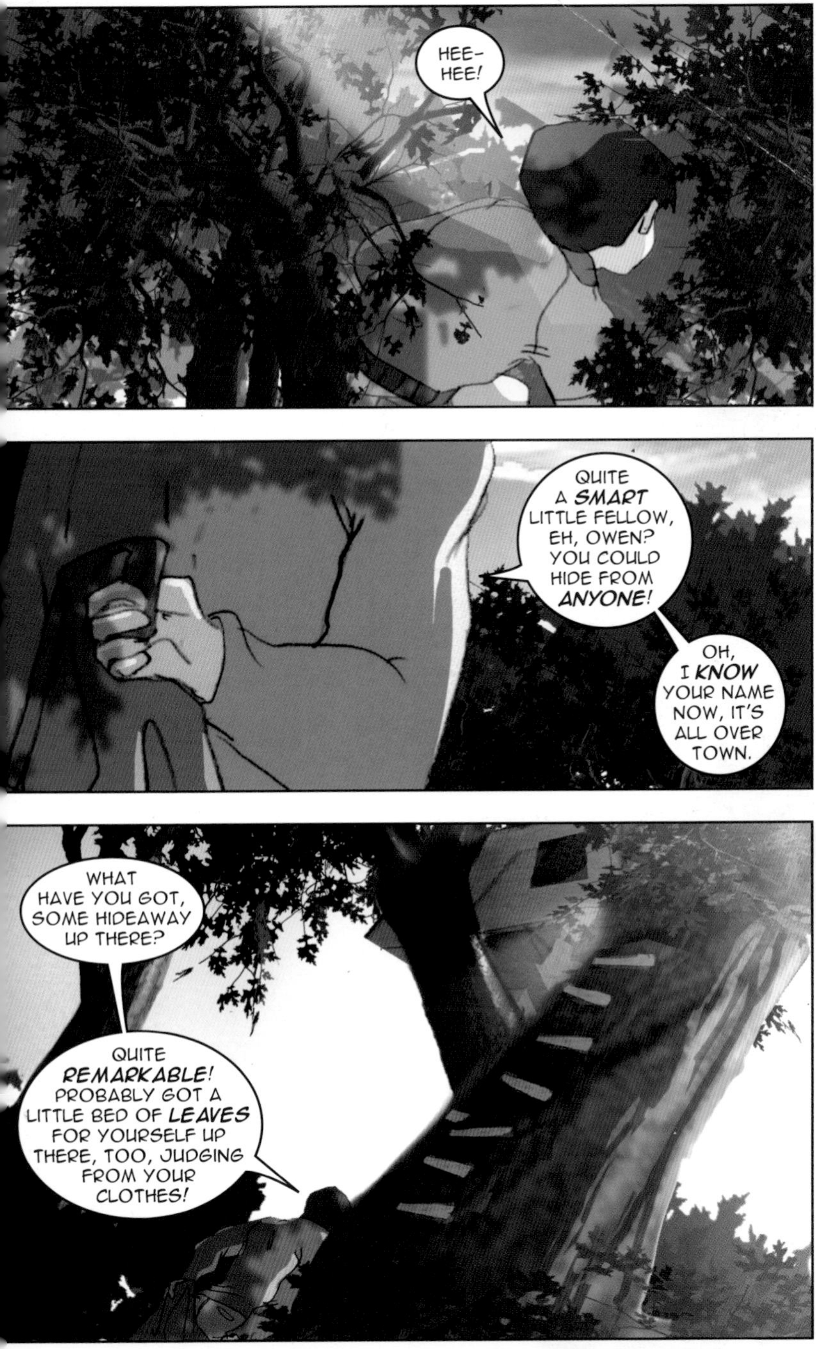
HEE-HEE!
QUITE A SMART LITTLE FELLOW, EH, OWEN? YOU COULD HIDE FROM ANYONE!
OH, I KNOW YOUR NAME NOW, IT'S ALL OVER TOWN.
WHAT HAVE YOU GOT, SOME HIDEAWAY UP THERE?
QUITE REMARKABLE! PROBABLY GOT A LITTLE BED OF LEAVES FOR YOURSELF UP THERE, TOO, JUDGING FROM YOUR CLOTHES!

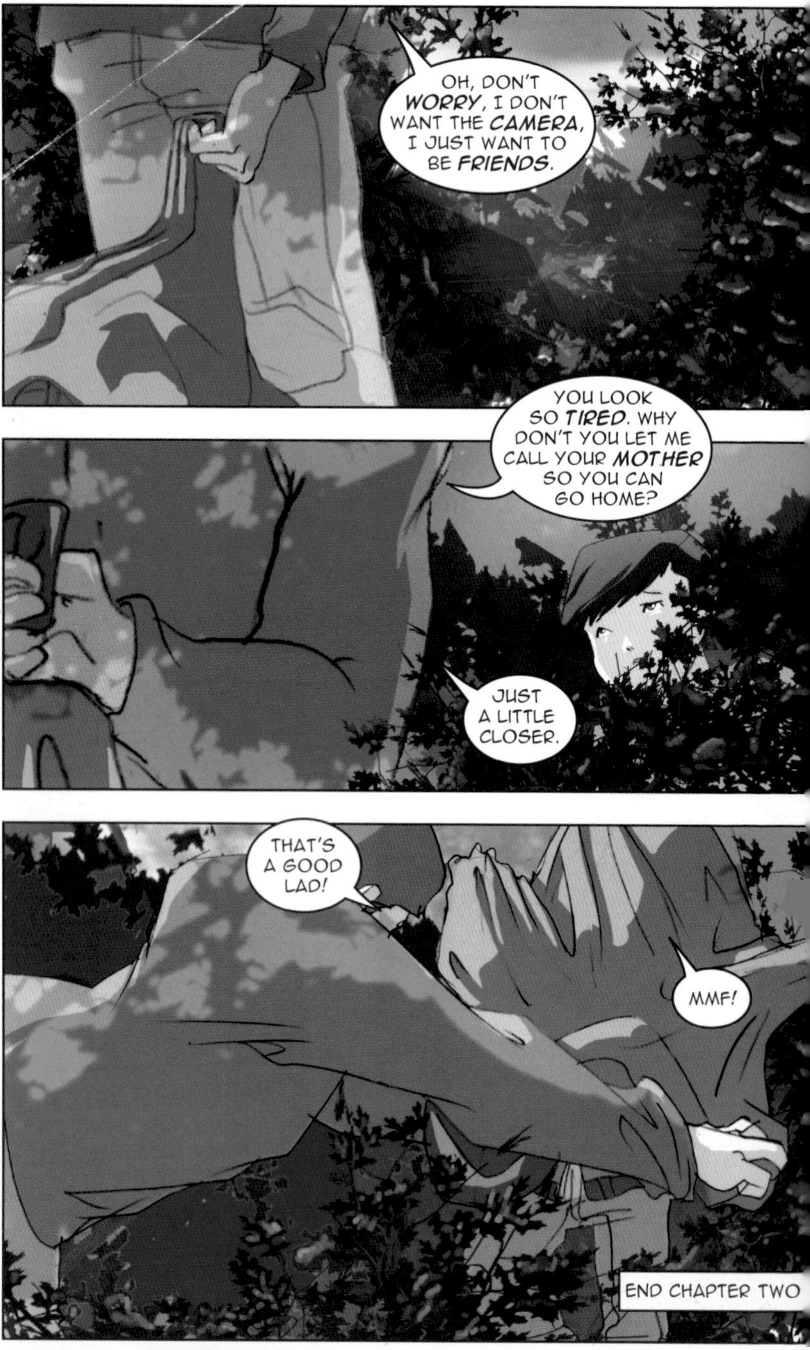
OH, DON'T WORRY, I DON'T WANT THE CAMERA, I JUST WANT TO BE FRIENDS.
YOU LOOK SO TIRED. WHY DON'T YOU LET ME CALL YOUR MOTHER SO YOU CAN GO HOME?
JUST A LITTLE CLOSER.
THAT'S A GOOD LAD!
MMF!
END CHAPTER TWO

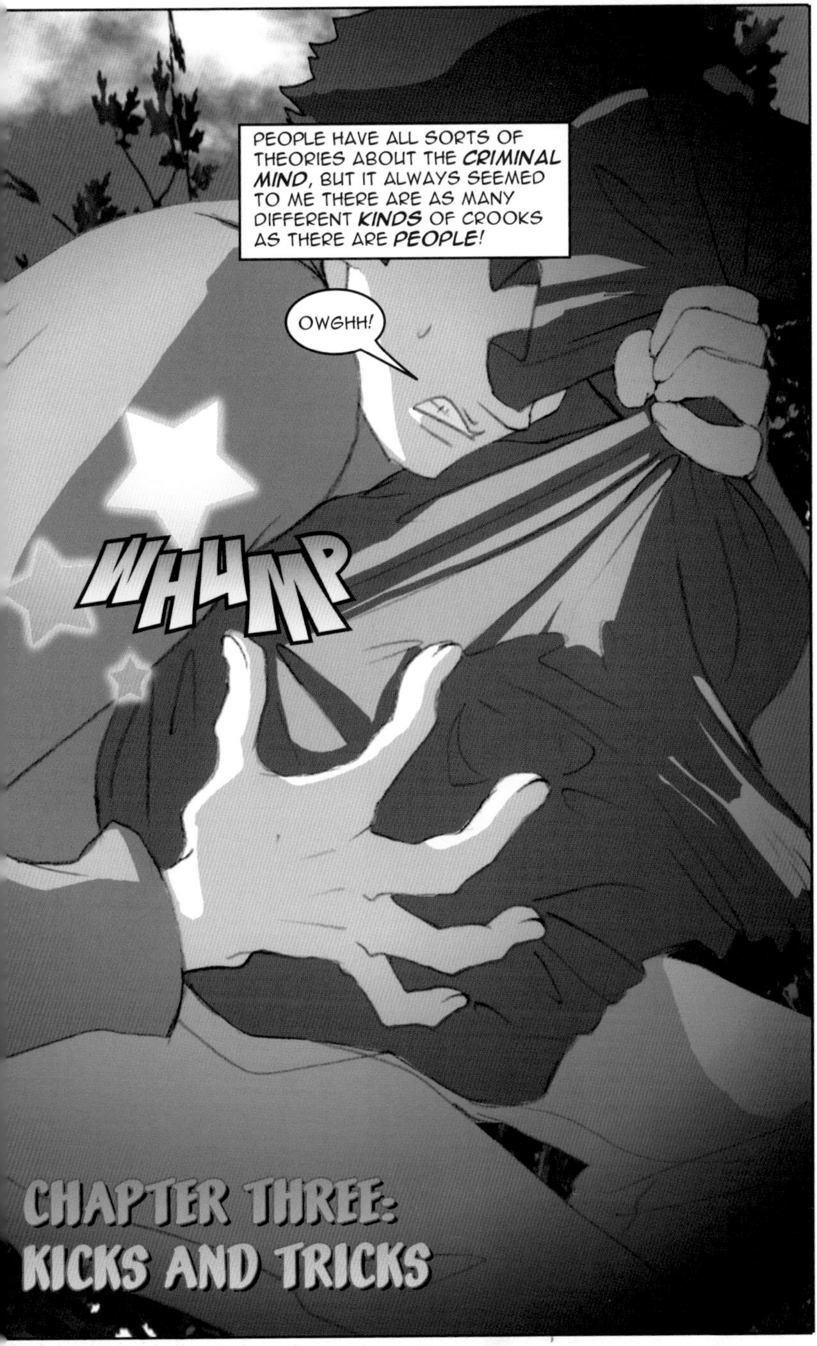
PEOPLE HAVE ALL SORTS OF THEORIES ABOUT THE CRIMINAL MIND, BUT IT ALWAYS SEEMED TO ME THERE ARE AS MANY DIFFERENT KINDS OF CROOKS AS THERE ARE PEOPLE!
OWGHH!
WHUMP
CHAPTER THREE:
KICKS AND TRICKS

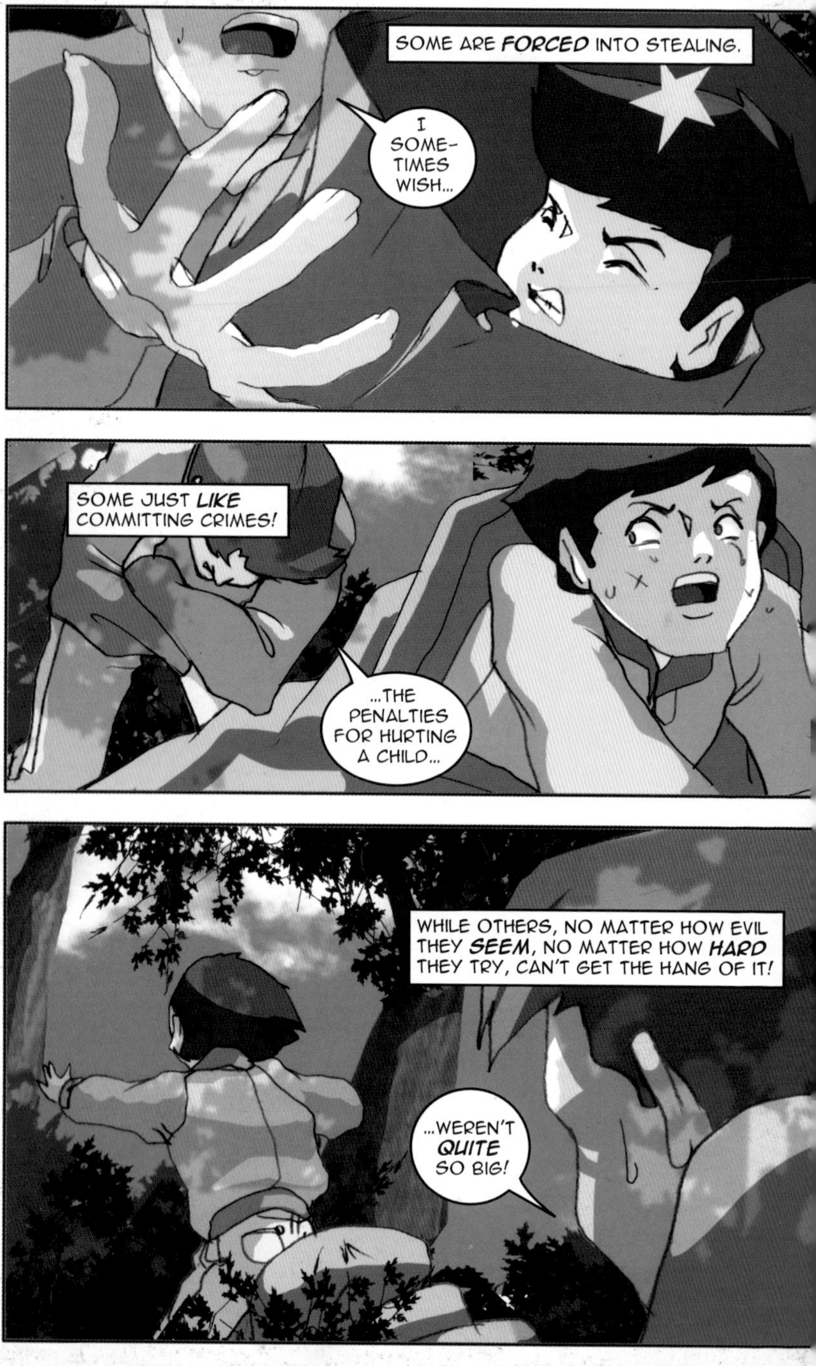
SOME ARE FORCED INTO STEALING.
I SOMETIMES WISH...
SOME JUST LIKE COMMITTING CRIMES!
...THE PENALTIES FOR HURTING A CHILD...
WHILE OTHERS, NO MATTER HOW EVIL THEY SEEM, NO MATTER HOW HARD THEY TRY, CAN'T GET THE HANG OF IT!
...WEREN'T QUITE SO BIG!

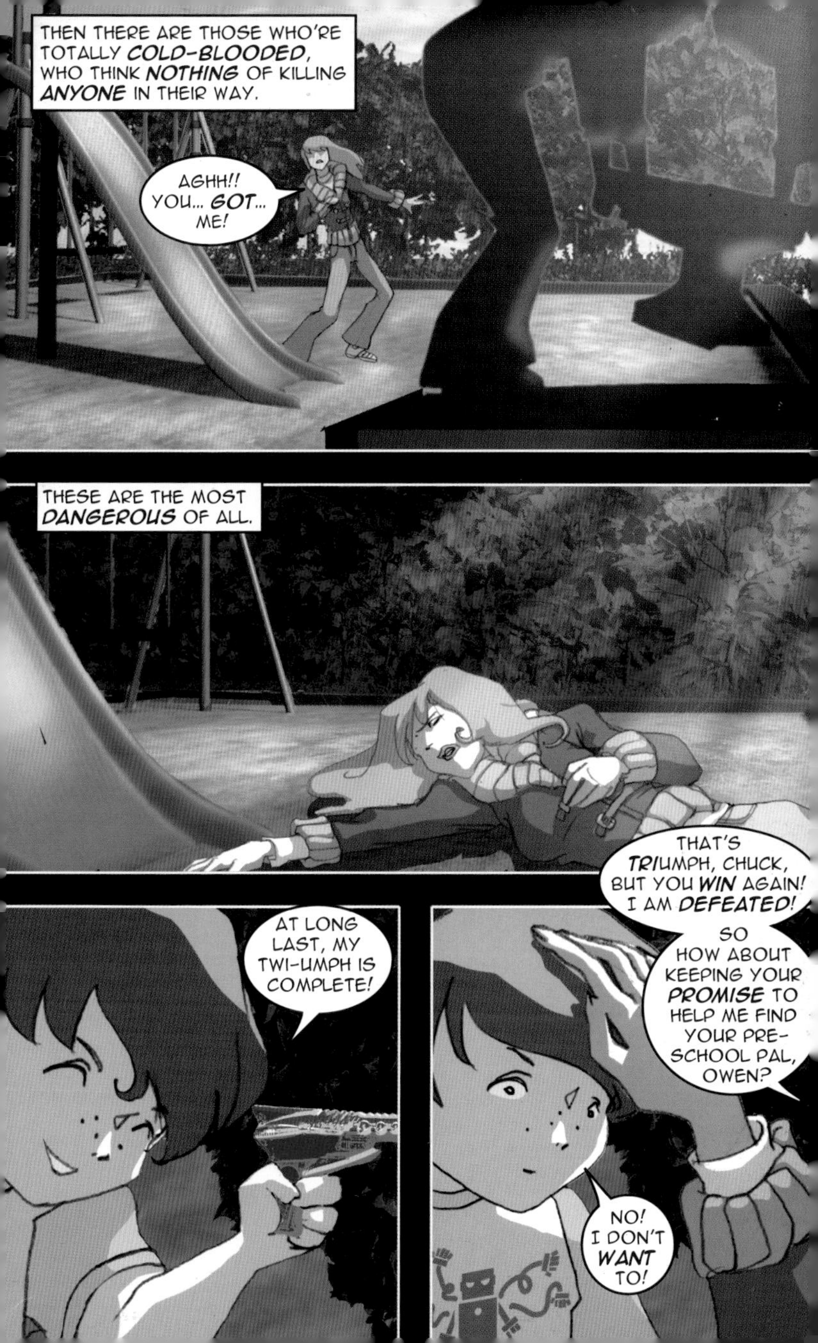

THEN THERE ARE THOSE WHO'RE TOTALLY COLD-BLOODED, WHO THINK NOTHING OF KILLING ANYONE IN THEIR WAY.
AGHH!! YOU... GOT... ME!
THESE ARE THE MOST DANGEROUS OF ALL.
AT LONG LAST, MY TWI-UMPH IS COMPLETE!
THAT'S TRIUMPH, CHUCK, BUT YOU WIN AGAIN! I AM DEFEATED!
SO HOW ABOUT KEEPING YOUR PROMISE TO HELP ME FIND YOUR PRE-SCHOOL PAL, OWEN?
NO! I DON'T WANT TO!

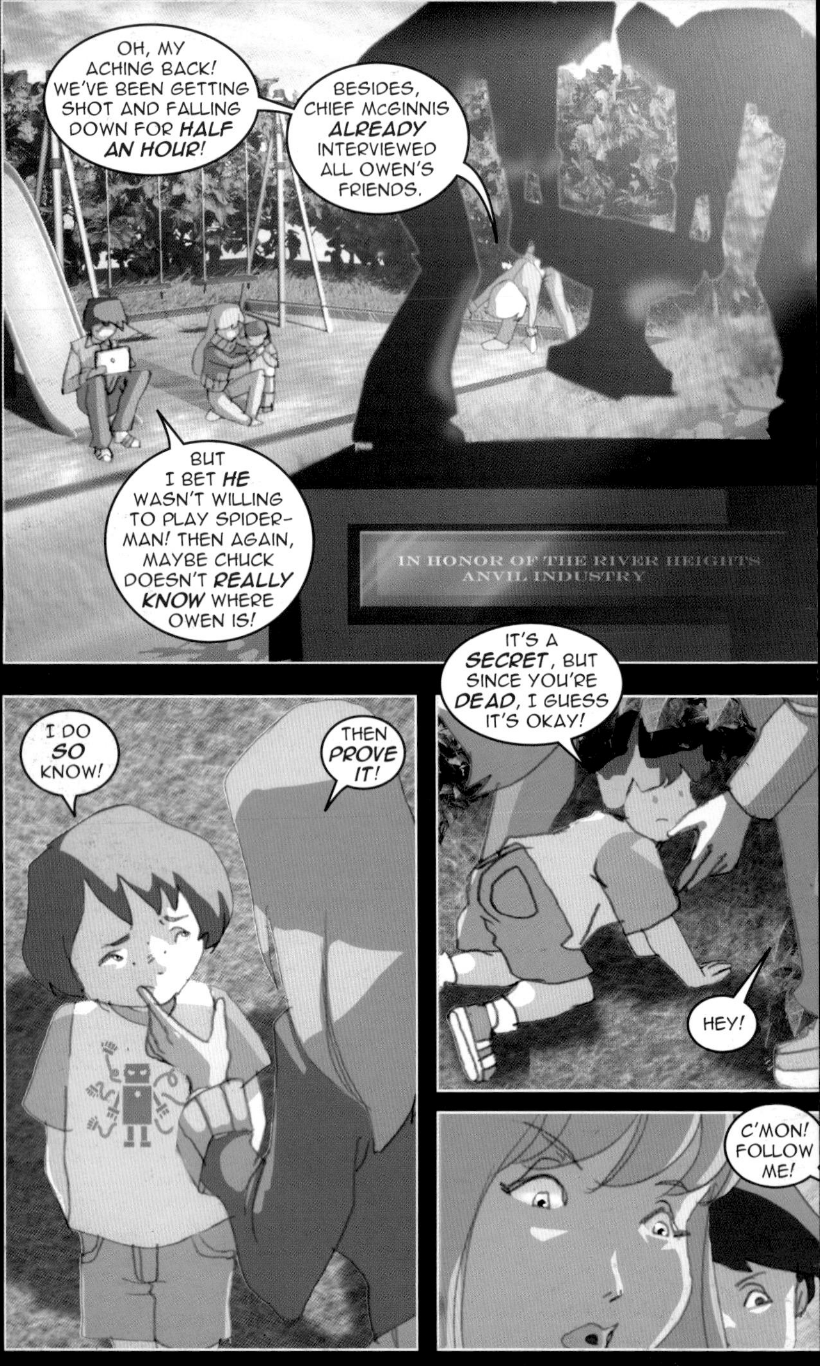

OH, MY ACHING BACK! WE'VE BEEN GETTING SHOT AND FALLING DOWN FOR HALF AN HOUR!
BESIDES, CHIEF McGINNIS ALREADY INTERVIEWED ALL OWEN'S FRIENDS.
BUT I BET HE WASN'T WILLING TO PLAY SPIDER-MAN! THEN AGAIN, MAYBE CHUCK DOESN'T REALLY KNOW WHERE OWEN IS!
IN HONOR OF THE RIVER HEIGHTS ANVIL INDUSTRY
I DO SO KNOW!
THEN PROVE IT!
IT'S A SECRET, BUT SINCE YOU'RE DEAD, I GUESS IT'S OKAY!
HEY!
C'MON! FOLLOW ME!

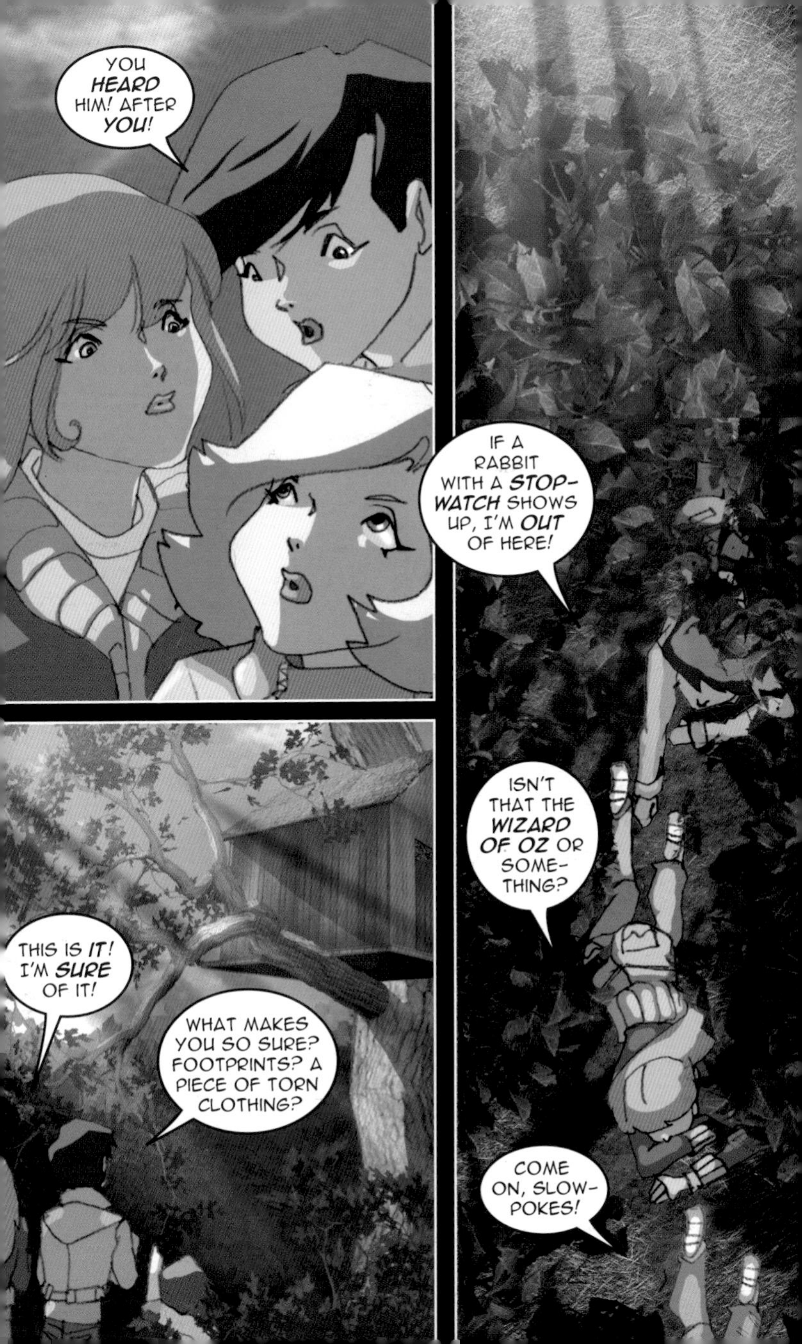
YOU HEARD HIM! AFTER YOU!
IF A RABBIT WITH A STOP-WATCH SHOWS UP, I'M OUT OF HERE!
ISN'T THAT THE WIZARD OF OZ OR SOME-THING?
COME ON, SLOW-POKES!
THIS IS IT! I'M SURE OF IT!
WHAT MAKES YOU SO SURE? FOOTPRINTS? A PIECE OF TORN CLOTHING?

Y'KNOW, MY BEING A **VEGETARIAN** REALLY HONES MY INVESTIGATIVE INTUITION, AND I SMELL SOMETHING'S **UP**!

THERE ISN'T ANYTHING YOU'RE **NOT** TELLING ME, RIGHT?

MARLETTA, EVERYTHING I SAID IS **ABSOLUTELY** TRUE!

YEAH, BUT WHAT I SAID **WASN'T** ABSOLUTELY **EVERYTHING** THAT WAS TRUE. LIKE, I FAILED TO MENTION THE **REASON** WE DIDN'T HAVE THE TAPE WAS BECAUSE IT WAS **ERASED**.

SO, NANCY, WE'D BETTER GET GOING... TO THAT **PLACE**... TO DO THAT **THING**, RIGHT?

RIGHT!

ER.... A PLACE FOR EVERY **THING**, AND A THING FOR EVERY **PLACE**, I ALWAYS SAY.

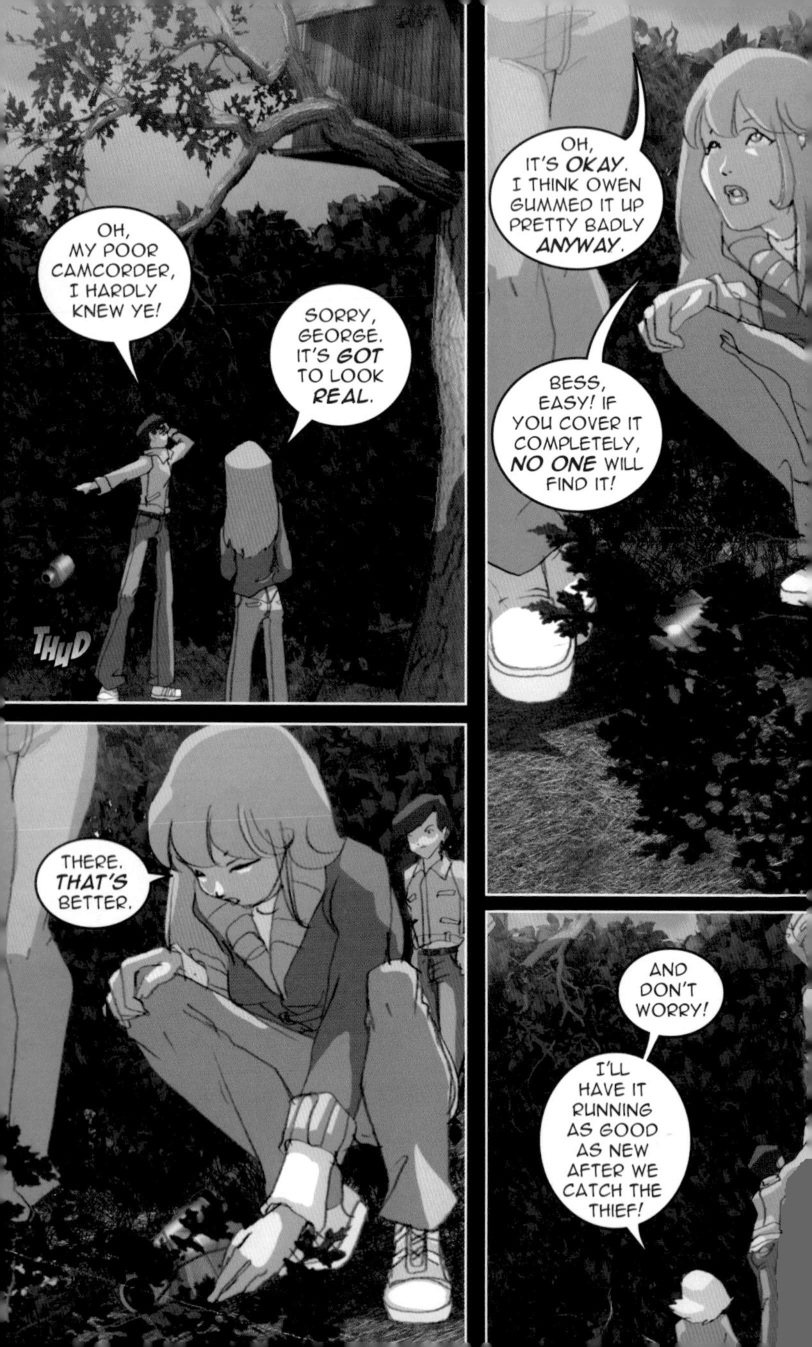
OH, MY POOR CAMCORDER, I HARDLY KNEW YE!
SORRY, GEORGE. IT'S *GOT* TO LOOK *REAL*.
THUD
OH, IT'S *OKAY*. I THINK OWEN GUMMED IT UP PRETTY BADLY *ANYWAY*.
BESS, EASY! IF YOU COVER IT COMPLETELY, *NO ONE* WILL FIND IT!
THERE. *THAT'S* BETTER.
AND DON'T WORRY!
I'LL HAVE IT RUNNING AS GOOD AS NEW AFTER WE CATCH THE THIEF!

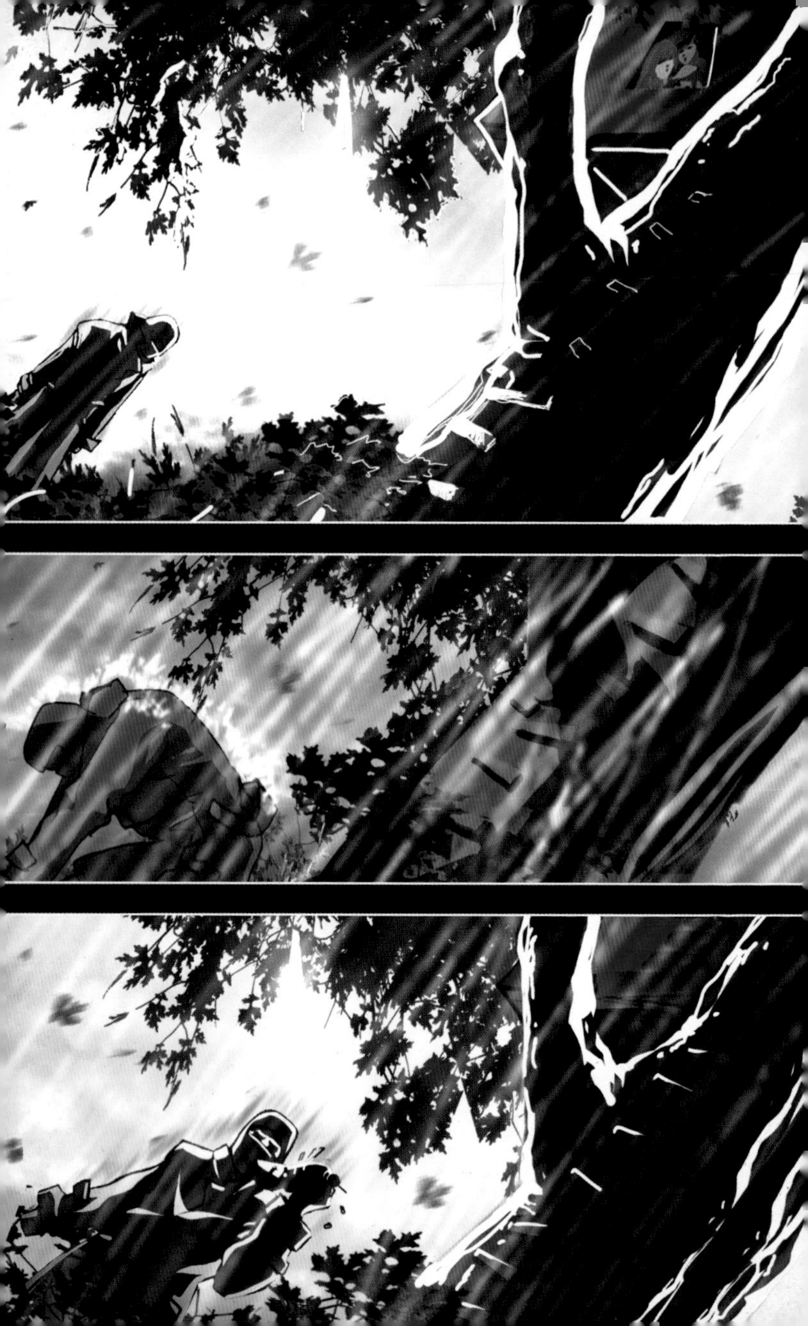

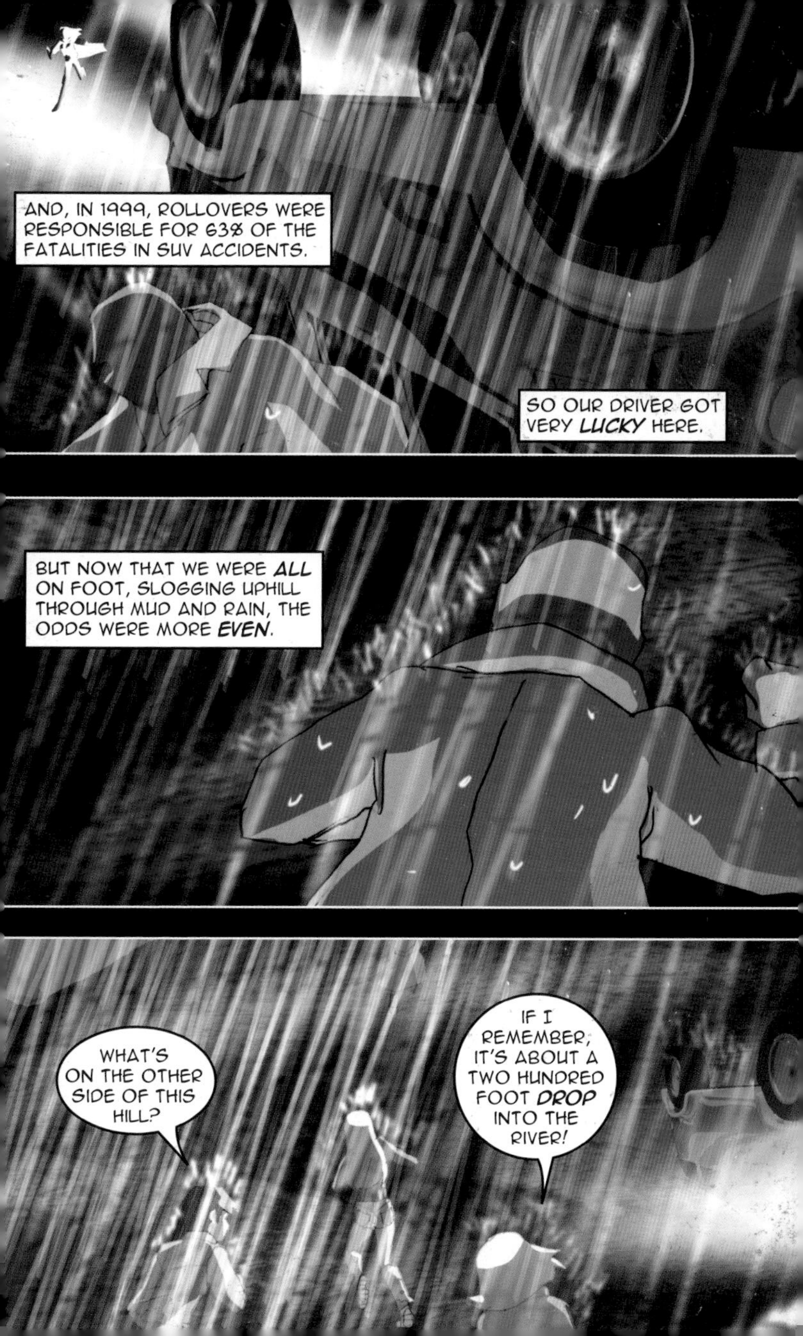
AND, IN 1999, ROLLOVERS WERE RESPONSIBLE FOR 63% OF THE FATALITIES IN SUV ACCIDENTS.
SO OUR DRIVER GOT VERY LUCKY HERE.
BUT NOW THAT WE WERE ALL ON FOOT, SLOGGING UPHILL THROUGH MUD AND RAIN, THE ODDS WERE MORE EVEN.
WHAT'S ON THE OTHER SIDE OF THIS HILL?
IF I REMEMBER, IT'S ABOUT A TWO HUNDRED FOOT DROP INTO THE RIVER!

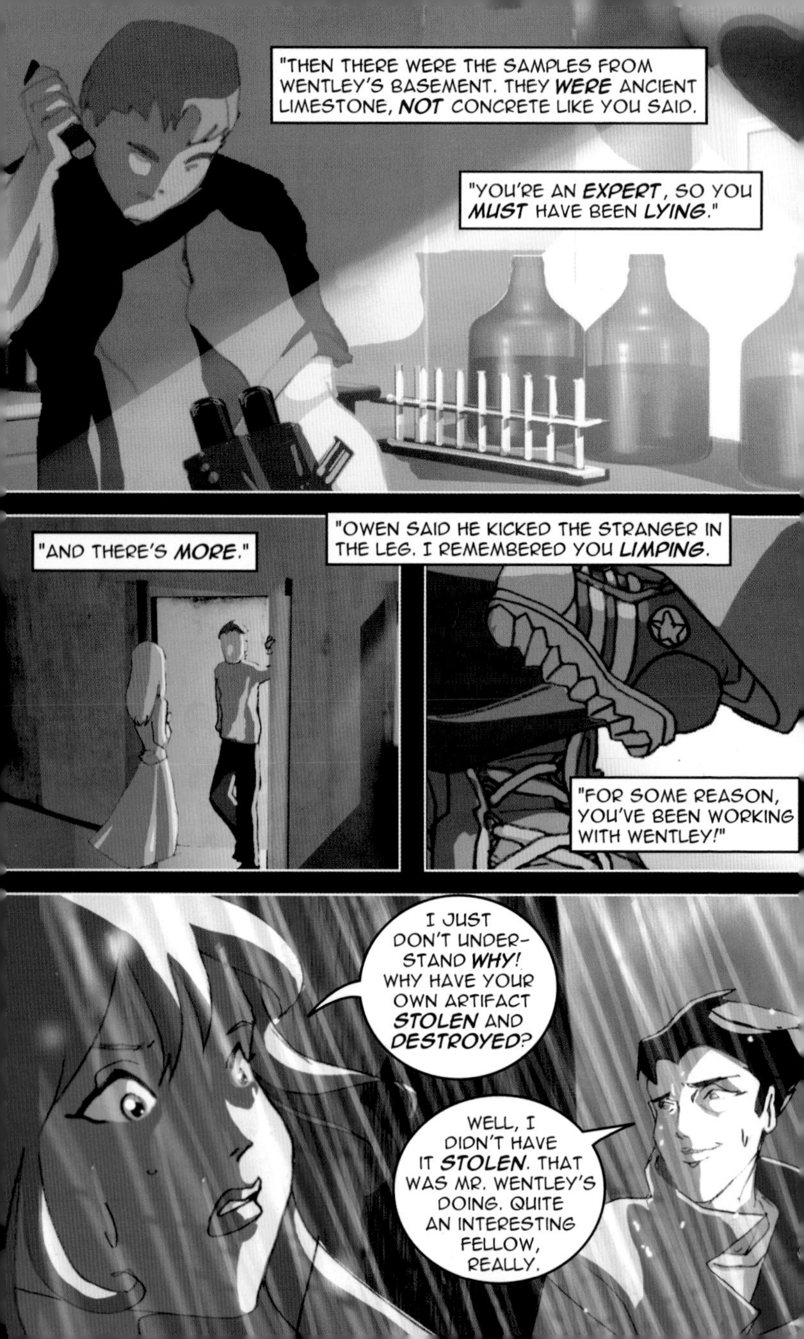
"THEN THERE WERE THE SAMPLES FROM WENTLEY'S BASEMENT. THEY WERE ANCIENT LIMESTONE, NOT CONCRETE LIKE YOU SAID.
"YOU'RE AN EXPERT, SO YOU MUST HAVE BEEN LYING."
"AND THERE'S MORE."
"OWEN SAID HE KICKED THE STRANGER IN THE LEG. I REMEMBERED YOU LIMPING.
"FOR SOME REASON, YOU'VE BEEN WORKING WITH WENTLEY!"
I JUST DON'T UNDER-STAND WHY! WHY HAVE YOUR OWN ARTIFACT STOLEN AND DESTROYED?
WELL, I DIDN'T HAVE IT STOLEN. THAT WAS MR. WENTLEY'S DOING. QUITE AN INTERESTING FELLOW, REALLY.

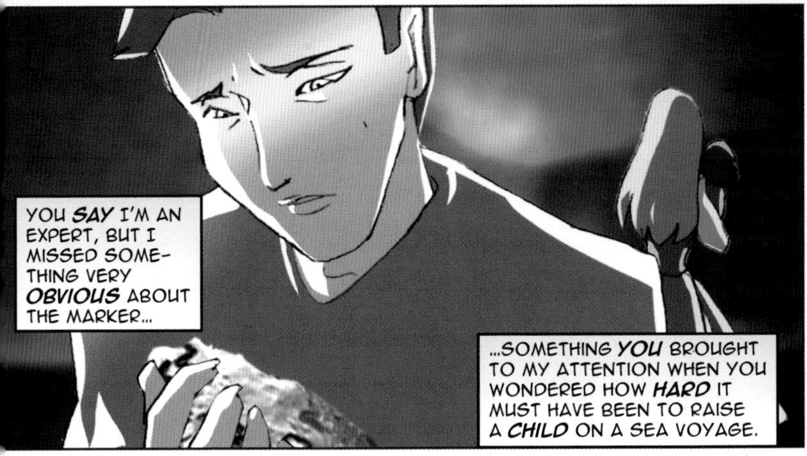
YOU SAY I'M AN EXPERT, BUT I MISSED SOME-THING VERY OBVIOUS ABOUT THE MARKER...
...SOMETHING YOU BROUGHT TO MY ATTENTION WHEN YOU WONDERED HOW HARD IT MUST HAVE BEEN TO RAISE A CHILD ON A SEA VOYAGE.

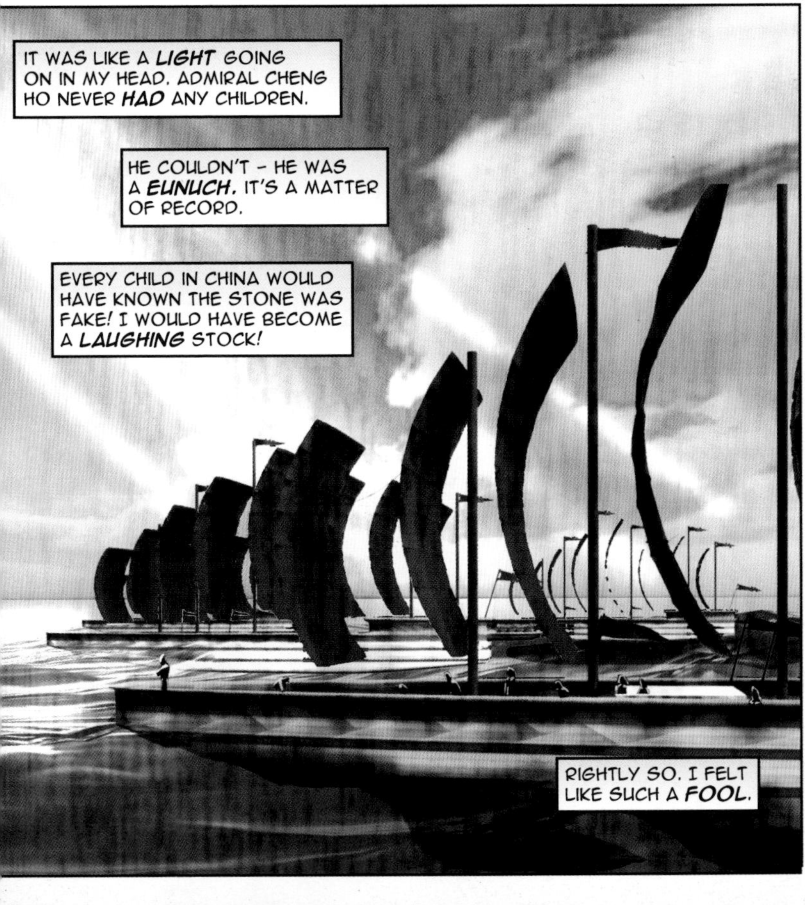
IT WAS LIKE A LIGHT GOING ON IN MY HEAD. ADMIRAL CHENG HO NEVER HAD ANY CHILDREN.
HE COULDN'T - HE WAS A EUNUCH. IT'S A MATTER OF RECORD.
EVERY CHILD IN CHINA WOULD HAVE KNOWN THE STONE WAS FAKE! I WOULD HAVE BECOME A LAUGHING STOCK!
RIGHTLY SO. I FELT LIKE SUCH A FOOL.

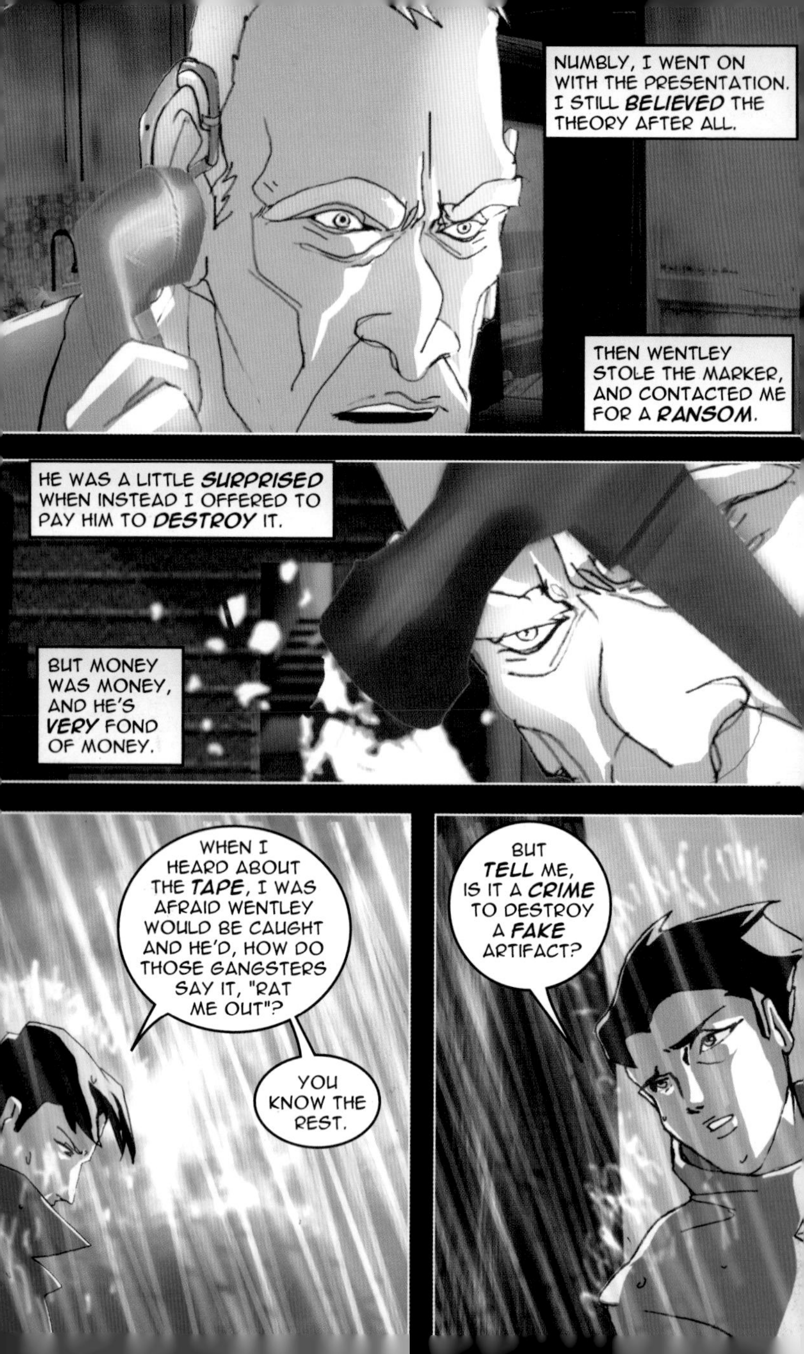
NUMBLY, I WENT ON WITH THE PRESENTATION. I STILL *BELIEVED* THE THEORY AFTER ALL.
THEN WENTLEY STOLE THE MARKER, AND CONTACTED ME FOR A *RANSOM*.
HE WAS A LITTLE *SURPRISED* WHEN INSTEAD I OFFERED TO PAY HIM TO *DESTROY* IT.
BUT MONEY WAS MONEY, AND HE'S *VERY* FOND OF MONEY.
WHEN I HEARD ABOUT THE *TAPE*, I WAS AFRAID WENTLEY WOULD BE CAUGHT AND HE'D, HOW DO THOSE GANGSTERS SAY IT, "RAT ME OUT"?
YOU KNOW THE REST.
BUT *TELL* ME, IS IT A *CRIME* TO DESTROY A *FAKE* ARTIFACT?

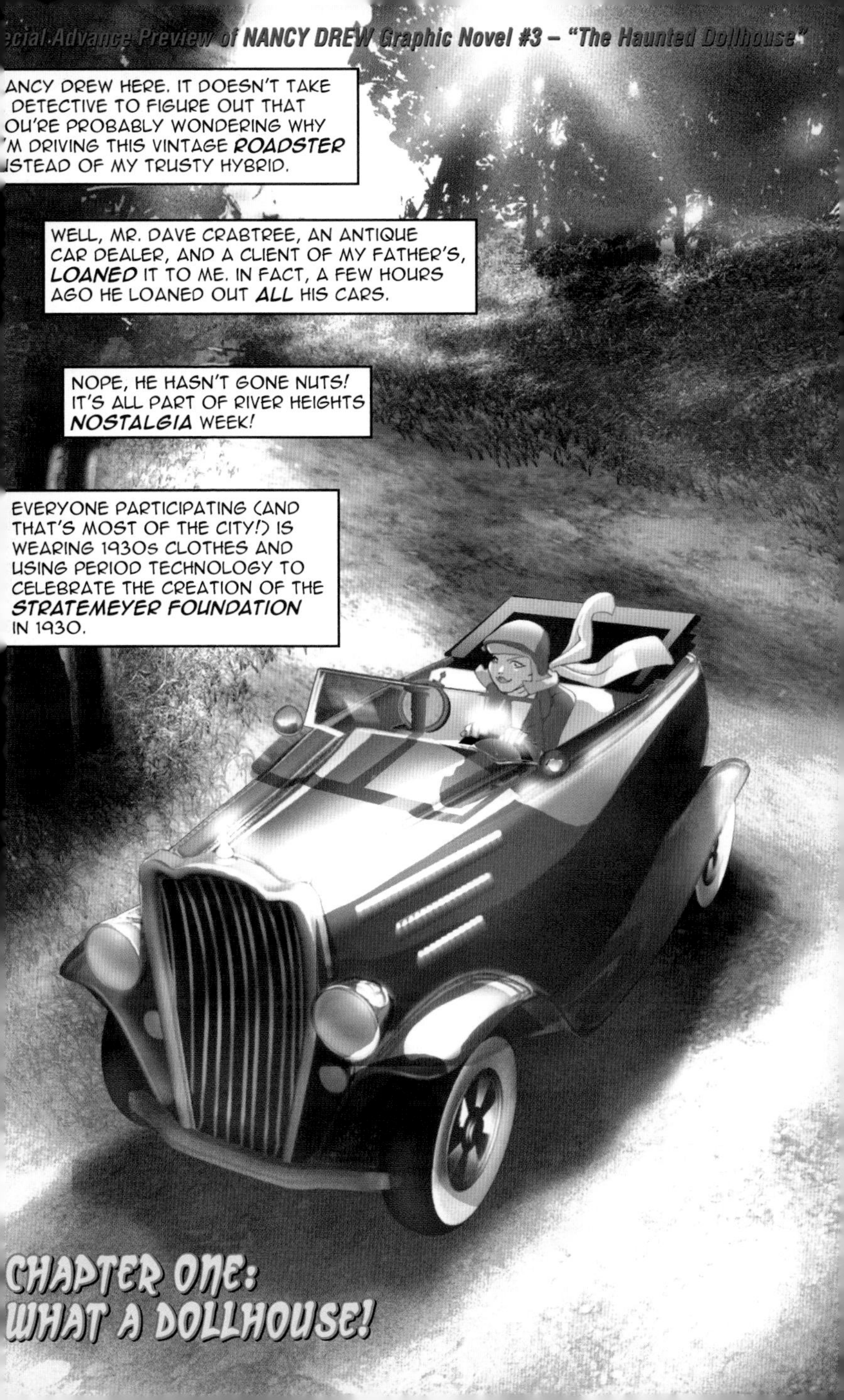

ANCY DREW HERE. IT DOESN'T TAKE DETECTIVE TO FIGURE OUT THAT OU'RE PROBABLY WONDERING WHY 'M DRIVING THIS VINTAGE ROADSTER ISTEAD OF MY TRUSTY HYBRID.
WELL, MR. DAVE CRABTREE, AN ANTIQUE CAR DEALER, AND A CLIENT OF MY FATHER'S, LOANED IT TO ME. IN FACT, A FEW HOURS AGO HE LOANED OUT ALL HIS CARS.
NOPE, HE HASN'T GONE NUTS! IT'S ALL PART OF RIVER HEIGHTS NOSTALGIA WEEK!
EVERYONE PARTICIPATING (AND THAT'S MOST OF THE CITY!) IS WEARING 1930s CLOTHES AND USING PERIOD TECHNOLOGY TO CELEBRATE THE CREATION OF THE STRATEMEYER FOUNDATION IN 1930.
CHAPTER ONE: WHAT A DOLLHOUSE!

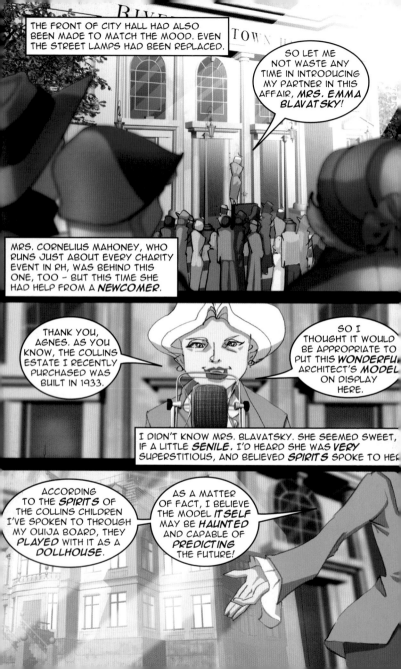

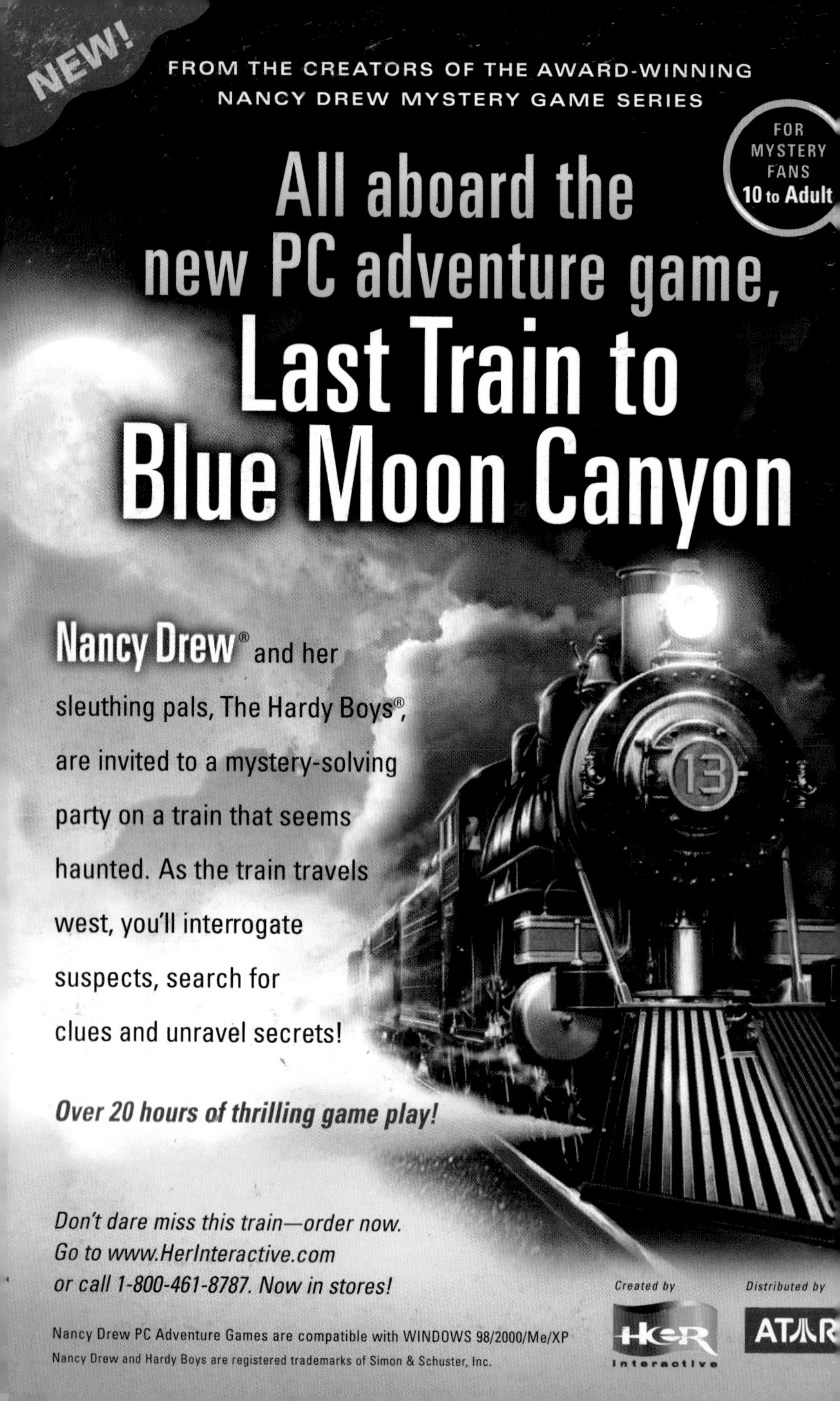

NEW!
FROM THE CREATORS OF THE AWARD-WINNING NANCY DREW MYSTERY GAME SERIES
FOR MYSTERY FANS 10 to Adult
All aboard the new PC adventure game,
Last Train to Blue Moon Canyon
Nancy Drew® and her sleuthing pals, The Hardy Boys®, are invited to a mystery-solving party on a train that seems haunted. As the train travels west, you'll interrogate suspects, search for clues and unravel secrets!
Over 20 hours of thrilling game play!
Don't dare miss this train—order now.
Go to www.HerInteractive.com
or call 1-800-461-8787. Now in stores!
13
Created by
HER Interactive
Distributed by
ATARI
Nancy Drew PC Adventure Games are compatible with WINDOWS 98/2000/Me/XP
Nancy Drew and Hardy Boys are registered trademarks of Simon & Schuster, Inc.

Z
ALL NEW STORY ALL NEW GRAPHIC NOVEL
THE HARDY BOYS ®
#3
MAD HOUSE
UNDERCOVER BROTHERS™
Scott LOBDELL
Daniel RENDON
based on the novels
of Franklin W. Dixon
MaD HouSE
PAPERCUTZ

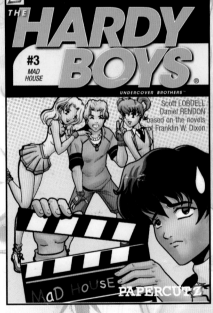